The Evershaw Curse

Jane Bond

V.R. Tapscott

This is a work of fiction. Names, characters, businesses, places, events, locales, and incidents are either the products of the author's imagination or used in a fictitious manner. Any resemblance to actual persons, living or dead, or actual events is purely coincidental.

Copyright 2021. All Rights Reserved. No portion of this book may be reproduced in any form without permission from the publisher, except as permitted by US copyright law. For permissions contact: vrtapscott@electrikink.com

Dedication

Thanks to all the people (hey, that's you I'm talking about!) who've read Jane's stories so far.

Thanks so much to my friend Seth and to my wife, they both helped with trying to make sure this all hung together and didn't sound too silly! If it still does, it's not their fault – they tried!

Thanks again to my friend Jax. Jax taught me that pain is part of life, and pain makes for good stories.

Thanks to my dad and mom, who have done more than anyone else to bring me to here.

And, because I can, thanks to VooDoo Doughnuts in Portland OR and Glaze Donuts in Wenatchee, WA. You guys rock!

The Evershaw Curse

The Jane Bond Series

Jane Bond – Some Assembly Required
Jane Bond – Dark Side of the Moon
Jane Bond – Moons of Jupiter
Jane Bond – The Case of the Evershaw Curse

Jane Bond – On Audible Audiobooks

The Lacey & Alex Series

Lacey & Alex and the Dagger of Ill Repute
Lacey & Alex - A Whole New World
(Coming February '21)

[Amazon's V.R. Tapscott Page](#)
[VRTapscott's Facebook Page](#)
[Sign up for Jane's Newsletter](#)

V.R. Tapscott

Contents

Appetizers 8
Chapter One 20
Chapter Two 29
Chapter Three 37
Chapter Four 43
Chapter Five 50
Chapter Six 65
Chapter Seven 72
Chapter Eight 78
Chapter Nine 85
Chapter Ten 94
Chapter Eleven 100
Chapter Twelve 105
Chapter Thirteen 108
Chapter Fourteen 111
Chapter Fifteen 118
Chapter Sixteen 121
Chapter Seventeen 129
Chapter Eighteen 139

Chapter Nineteen...145
Chapter Twenty 151
Chapter Twenty-One..158
Chapter Twenty-Two 160
Chapter Twenty-Three..167
Chapter Twenty-Four..174
Chapter Twenty-Five 184
Chapter Twenty-Six...192
Chapter Twenty-Seven 199
Chapter Twenty-Eight...203
Chapter Twenty-Nine 209
Chapter Thirty...218
Chapter Thirty-One 222
Chapter Thirty-Two...228
Chapter Thirty-Three 231
Chapter Thirty-Four..236
Excerpt – Lacey & Alex and the Dagger of Ill Repute...............239

V.R. Tapscott

Appetizers

Jane

I pulled Threepio to a stop in the small parking lot, slotting in between a classic BMW and a brand-new Volkswagen. Since Threepio is an ancient Venture van from the late 90s, he didn't necessarily fit in here, however I told him to buck up and feel right, he had it over those cars every time. He seemed to be mollified by this idea. I pulled down the tiny vanity mirror and gave myself a cursory look. I'm not really into the whole fashion thing too much, but I have to admit that going someplace with Georgia's friends there made me a little antsy. I like Georgia, but she's in a different world when it comes to her acquaintances.

I pushed my bright red hair around a bit, checked for broccoli in my teeth, made sure my modicum of lipstick hadn't managed to take a beachhead on my incisors, and finally realized I was just putting off getting out of the car.

The Evershaw Curse

I got out of the car.

I walked up to the tall redwood fence and pushed the button. I could hear a bell bingle-bong in the distance and flashed on the memory of WKRP's Jennifer and her fancy doorbell. Come to think of it, her co-worker at WKRP had been Bailey. Small world.

The gate opened slowly, and I backed up a few feet. I was a bit struck dumb. The Adonis who opened the gate was about six feet tall, tan, blue eyes, blonde hair, and completely naked. Nude. Stripped. In a clothing optional condition.

I have to admit all my synapses stopped firing. Or maybe all of them were firing at once. At any rate, my jaw dropped open a bit, and I probably looked like a lunatic. Of course, I suppose anyone that looked that good AND went around sans clothing was probably used to it.

He smiled. "You must be Jane. Georgia said you'd be coming up; I've been so looking forward to meeting you!"

My jaw finally unfroze, and I looked at him right in the eye. Since, for one thing, looking anywhere else would cause my jaw to lock again, I figured.

He laughed. "I take it Georgia didn't tell you her guest policy?"

I shook my head.

He shook his head too. "I suppose it's a joke, to her. Either that or she just really doesn't think about it. Which is entirely possible. I mean, considering how many times she has to strip out of whatever she's wearing and start over again, it must be a hazard of the job." He appeared to stop and think a moment. "Or a perk, I guess."

He seemed to suddenly realize I was still standing there, gaping.

"Come on in, Jane, take off your clothes and get comfortable. Once you're dressed like the rest of us, you'll feel much better!"

My brain had unfrozen enough to have a thought skitter through - that in this instance, saying "Oh, I didn't bring anything to wear" was a complete non-starter. In fact, the very definition of the "guest policy" was exactly that. Nothing to wear.

"I don't think… I mean, I don't have any… er… I mean, I'm not prepared."

He smiled indulgently. "That's the great advantage to Georgia's house, no one ever has to worry about wearing the right thing."

Georgia's voice came from across the lawn, and I saw her in all her glory, walking this way. "Come on, leave her alone, Jack. She doesn't need any help getting undressed."

He snorted. "Maybe, but I'm not sure she can even move, alone."

"If you step away from her a few paces, or go back to the deck, I have a feeling she'll be fine. After all, she's seen ME, before."

He shrugged. "Ok."

With that he walked away, and contrary to what Georgia had said, it was just as distracting and jaw freezing to watch him walk away. I was suddenly aware of Georgia's hand being passed in front of my eyes, and the "Earth to Jane, come in Jane" mantra she was humming. Also, "Dale. Remember Dale."

I snapped at her. "I remember Dale, but I also know that he's just as susceptible to you as… as I am to Jack."

I stuck my tongue out at her for good measure. Can't let her get the upper hand.

I continued, "You might have told me that this was going to be a clothing optional visit when you invited me to stay a few days at your house."

She smirked. "Why take the fun out of it?"

She had me there, and I probably deserved it.

"Are you really expecting that I'll be running around in the buff the next couple days, Georgia? Are you kidding me?"

Once again showing off the assets that were paying for this compound, she shrugged. "Not really. I figured once you get naked, you'll get comfortable with it."

I sighed. "I don't suppose you have a changing room?"

She giggled. "A changing room in a nudist colony? Isn't there something kind of odd about that concept?"

I looked at her grimly. "No."

She gave in. "The bathrooms are over in that little building there. I suppose you could call them changing rooms if you want. Just remember that the common area is gender neutral!"

I stared at her for a minute, then sighed and started stripping.

It was her turn for the jaw drop thing, then she giggled again and said, "I swear, Jane, you're always a surprise."

Taking the last stitch off wasn't as hard as I thought it was going to be. Since Georgia was there, already starkers, and Jack had kind of numbed me to the concept, I was matching her in a few minutes.

"I suppose you have tanning lotion?"

"Of course, we buy it by the case." She motioned toward the aforementioned bathrooms. "Showers, towels and lotions of all kinds in there. All kinds." She winked. "Bring Dale next time."

In the end, it was a great weekend, I got a lot of tan (loosely translates to 'lots of tiny freckles') in places that I'd never tanned before and found out some interesting information. Like, don't cook pancakes, or especially eggs, without an apron.

I also decided that there was no way in Hell that Dale would be accompanying me next time. Georgia's friends were just too good-looking, and I was too nice a person to expose Dale's heart to that kind of palpitations. And yes, that's the only reason.

Olive

The Evershaw Curse

live stepped out of her little car. She'd popped into a dark underground parking lot and then driven the last few miles for show. Her little smart car had been upgraded, she'd fallen so much in love with Jane's Saturn Sky that she got one for herself, only of course, hers was bright red. Uncharacteristically unsure of herself, she got out of the car and started walking. She'd chosen a good day. It was bright and sunny, and the sky as blue as a Montana morning. Portland wasn't always that blue, in fact, a cloudy grey was more its style.

She wandered along the sidewalk, just enjoying the exposed aggregate while watching the cars. Of course, she was also watching out for the cars, half expecting to be run over. For all her playacting, sometimes she felt like a little kid inside and turned on the aggressiveness of her sometimes-nasty tongue out of self-defense. Or just because she was feeling snarky, of course.

Today though, was a day for introspection, and Olive wanted to soak in the feeling of being in a big city. She'd tried to bond with Seattle, but for some reason it never clicked. Of course, it might just be that Seattle didn't have any VooDoo Doughnuts. And Olive was in love with the whole idea of VooDoo Doughnuts.

To that end, she arrived at said donut shop. Today, almost sadly, there was no line outside and she was able to go in and absorb the smells and the general feel of the little shop. For once, there was no clamor, no bustle. She giggled a little as she picked out a voodoo doll donut. No, of course, that wasn't all. She picked out a dozen donuts all told, making sure to get at least one maple-bacon bar, Jane's favorite.

She pondered for a moment, wondering if she could, or more to the point, if she should modify the parameters of Jane's nanobots to jump Jane's metabolism a little and make sure the donut didn't cause any weight gain. Jane had no idea, and Olive had no intention of telling her, that Olive had that much control over Jane's internal workings. Regretfully, she decided that for now, she'd let Jane's system alone and let Jane decide what amount of weight gain was acceptable. In the past few months, it seemed that Jane was going to the gym all the time. That was causing her to have a bit of an unhealthy obsession with fitness. Anything can be taken too far. Olive would watch the results of the next few weeks and decide how things should be tweaked, or if they should be. Olive loved Jane, and loved watching over her, making sure she was okay.

Meanwhile, she pointed out her choices and the girl behind the counter packed the box for her. Janus was another reason for her slight donut obsession. Today Janus had a whole row of tiny eyebrow ringlets above her left eyebrow and a truly stunning ruby in her left earlobe. Her right eyebrow and ear were left naked of embellishment. Olive grinned at Janus and got a saucy grin back. She pointed at her hair, which today matched Janus's white-hot look. They both nodded and grinned at each other like a couple of back-window doggies through the display glass, as Olive filled her dozen.

Arriving at the checkout counter, Janus said, "Hi Olive. How ya doin'?"

Olive drawled "Ah'm fine, darlin. You look good today! And every day."

Janus snorted, "Uh huh. Tell that to my old man."

Olive smirked. "Maybe you should dump 'im and pick me, pick me!"

Janus looked at her speculatively. "Maybe. Maybe so. It's something to consider." She gave Olive a big bawdy wink, which gave Olive goose bumps. "Twenty-three twenty, hon."

Olive stuck her black card in the slot and added a ridiculously large tip.

She walked back outside and wandered a few blocks, stopping to grab a big takeout cup of Stumptown coffee, and then hauling her box of donuts and the coffee along with her to the Skidmore Fountain, where she reverently placed the donut box on a bench and then joined it. She hauled out the voodoo doll donut and started eating it, sipping at the coffee, and just enjoying life. Jane was right, it's always good to be human.

While the fountain was silent, the birds made noise and the city around her made noise. Sometimes it was a gentle soothing roar, and sometimes it was a screeching cacophony, but it was always the city, and Olive loved it.

Later, as the afternoon waned, Olive began to feel just a little sick to her stomach. She'd tuned her system to simulate the human body as closely as she could, and apparently eight donuts were overkill for a human. She peered in the box and saw that she'd at least had the sense not to eat Jane's donut. Bailey'd just have to get along with one of the others. She looked at them again. Hm. Just one more…

She mentally slapped herself and stopped her hand moving toward the box mostly on its own. Maybe a little too human there, darlin.

She gathered up the donut box, deposited her cup in the recycle bin and set off for her car.

What a great day. What a great life.

Bailey

Bailey sighed a bit as she entered the foyer of the MGM Grand in Las Vegas. She'd been more or less banned from Vegas a couple years ago due to her unusually large winning streak. She'd been wined and dined and given a very large check for her winnings, and then politely asked to never come back.

Bailey being Bailey, there was a challenge in that particular gauntlet being thrown down. She'd always known she'd have to come back, if only to thumb her nose at that insufferable Carstead fellow.

The unspoken interior thought with that was that she might meet him in person. While he was an odious cretin, there was something about him that made her curious.

She sauntered around the Grand, taking in the sights as she went. She finally lit on Olive's favorite slot machine, the Planet Moolah one. She'd been feeding dollars into it at a frustrating rate for about 15 minutes, hardly getting a single jackpot, when a voice behind her spoke up.

"You seem to have lost your luck, Ms. Bailey."

Concentrating on the game, she jumped and knocked her purse flying, the contents of it spreading in an arc. She whipped around and, sure enough, it was Carstead. He at least had the grace to act sheepish.

With an irritated look at him, she spoke in a voice that would rival Grand Mof Tarkin of Star Wars fame, "I should have known it would be you, mister Carstead."

She bent to gather her belongings and her head met his with a crack, both of them knocked off kilter and winding up sitting on the floor. She looked daggers at him, but he looked so off balance and shocked that she started laughing. He seemed nonplussed for a moment, but then realized the silliness of their position and started to laugh too.

Still chuckling, they crawled around on the floor, gathering Bailey's possessions into an untidy pile in one location so she could put them back in her purse. Finally, she stood up and leaned back against the machine she'd been feeding and looked at him. Just as she opened her mouth to ask him what the hell he was doing scaring the crap out of paying customers, the machine she was sitting on began warbling its jackpot theme. Evidently, she'd left a play on it and had done some butt-gambling.

Bailey jumped away from the machine like it had stung her, watching in amazement as the numbers rolled up, doing pay after pay until the total stood at $28,000.

She quirked a smile at him, "You were saying, mister Carstead?"

He ran a palm down his face, finally staring at her and saying, "Obviously I was mistaken, Ms. Bailey. And please, call me James."

Bailey paused for a moment, looking at him. "All right, James. And since you insist on calling me 'Ms. Bailey' rather than 'Ms. McCallum', you can drop the 'Ms." and just make it Bailey."

He smiled a genuine smile. "I'd like that… erm… Bailey. Might I take you to dinner at one of our fine restaurants to celebrate your winnings?"

Surprising even herself, she said, "With pleasure, James."

The Evershaw Curse

Bailey had dressed for the occasion, but knowing Vegas a bit by now, she'd chosen far more carefully than a pair of murderous stiletto heels, so the relatively short walk to Bavette's Steakhouse was quite enjoyable and the company was stellar. It seemed after the ice was broken, James Carstead was an actual person rather than an automaton.

As much as Bailey loved her, Jane had never lived in the corporate world. It was refreshing to talk with someone who'd had some of the same experiences that she had, and they met on a level playing field.

A few drinks with dinner, some dancing at some very exclusive night spots, and Bailey never did quite make it back to her hotel that night…

V.R. Tapscott

Chapter One

Maundy Monday

Everyone seemed to have had an enjoyable weekend as Monday arrived. We all got in late, and I was sitting kicked back at my desk, with my feet up, just relaxing after a morning full of paperwork. Well, ok, two Excel spreadsheets and some spam mail. Still, who knew that being a detective would involve so much more paperwork than shooting!

I hauled out my shiny new private investigator card with some pride. I never got tired of looking at it. Between opening Bailey and Bond, and getting my investigator's license, it seemed like it had taken forever. Making it through all the courses and exams had been a real nightmare, but looking at the card made my toes tingle. Or maybe it was from sitting too long.

At any rate, I hoped I'd have some luck with talking to my fellow detectives. It seemed to go either way for fictional detectives, and I was wondering if I'd get the good cop treatment or the bad cop treatment. Whether my detective compatriots would see me as a comrade-in-arms, or the competition.

I dialed the phone and said, "Ms. Daship, please hold all my calls."

A voice came back, "What??"

"I said, please hold all my calls."

"I HEARD what you said, I just can't believe you said it!" There was a click as she hung up on me. I grinned.

I yelled, "Hey, Bailey, we need a new secretary!"

Bailey's voice floated out of her office, "I didn't know we had a secretary."

Olive's voice didn't exactly float out of her office so much as arrive, throw the silence to the ground and stomp on it, "We don't. I'm NOT your secretary!"

I yelled back, "Then who's gonna answer all my calls wh…"

I came to a sudden stop. There was a woman standing at my office door, looking puzzled.

I said. "Um."

Not my finest hour.

She said, "Is this the Bailey and Bond Detective Agency?"

I rallied and stood up. "Yes, it is. What may I do for you? Please, have a seat."

I made polite hand motions at the client chair, which had really only been used by Bailey as of yet.

Bailey yelled, "When are we going to lunch?"

I blushed, then whispered, "Close door." The door slid across, shutting out anything short of a force five hurricane. Or even Olive.

"Excuse me, it's been a slow morning."

The woman looked a little nonplussed, but then seemed to take it in stride. "I'm Naomi Evershaw. My husband Bart is missing, and I was told you might be willing to check into it for me."

I was wondering who in the world would have referred us, since as far as real work we'd mostly sat in the office eating chips and going to lunches. I'd been looking at paperwork this morning, but it was mostly for show, since the big mainframe (which was really only about three inches square) did all our computer work, and just spat out fake Excel sheets to make it look like one of us knew what we were doing.

"I see. How long has Bart been missing, Ms. Evershaw?"

"Seventeen years, six days, fourteen hours and..." she looked at her watch, "eight minutes."

"I... see."

She gave me a sad smile. "No, you probably don't. Most people think I'm crazy, keeping at it. But I know he didn't just walk away from me. I'm running out of detective agencies, but since I was in Chelan on vacation this year, I thought I'd check into this one."

I said, "No one will look into his disappearance?"

"Oh no, they're all willing. But after a few days of looking, they tell me they can't find him and the trail is too old, or some other excuse, and then they send me a bill. And then I never hear from them again. I don't understand it, I'm willing to pay. Anything, really."

She sounded so sad and pathetic, there wasn't any way I could tell her no. So, I didn't. I told her we'd look into it.

We had some real genuine client sheets on letterhead and everything, and all the paperwork to actually do our job, so I hunted it all down and got her to fill out the pertinent information about herself and Bart.

Finally, after getting all of her information filled in, I said, "Naomi, can you take me through the events that led up to the last time you saw Bart?"

She took a breath, sat back and said, "Of course. I've been over it so many times I can practically say it by rote."

I gave her an encouraging smile and said, "I'm sorry to have to make you walk through it again, but I think it's the best place to start."

She nodded and began.

"Bart and I were made for each other. I know that probably sounds silly to anyone that's not actually in the same movie as you, but it was just how it was…"

Naomi and Bart had flown into New York and spent a couple days there, wandering the streets and getting charged up with excitement. Naomi thought that nothing could match the euphoria of marrying her soulmate a few days before. However, she had to admit the mounting excitement... er... that is, the amount of excitement generated from being not only in New York but planning on leaving for Paris in a couple days, was intoxicating.

They had hot dogs from street vendors, with plenty of sauerkraut and onions. They had genuine New York bagels, and pizza from a little shop that was hardly even a hole in the wall. A memorable night exploring each other as a married couple, then another day walking through Central Park and other tourist things in the area, and then a relaxed time getting to LaGuardia before it all went crazy.

Bart believed in travelling light to make it faster going through security, and he seemed to be right about that. Naomi hadn't travelled much since the attacks on the World Trade Center, but the security was a nightmare even with Bart's insistence on the lack of luggage. The three hours of lead time they'd allowed was cutting it close by the time they fought through the maze, and they barely made it to the waiting area at the gate before their flight was called.

The flight itself was quite nice, with full meal service and a choice of very nice wines and snacks. The large, comfortable seats allowed them to get at least some semblance of sleep.

They stepped off the plane in Paris at the Charles de Gaulle airport. The obligatory lines were not that much of a problem since it was only 6am. Naomi wasn't completely sure that, even taking into account the six-hour difference between New York and Paris, made it a good idea. Bart, however, had a thing about early arrivals and had wanted to make sure they had a full day in Paris before actually having to check into their hotel. Naomi had thought it was a cute habit she'd be able to break him of after a few months of training, but meanwhile, it actually did give them a full day in Paris. Of course, it was at the expense of a full night of flying. Thank goodness for her insistence on first class for the nearly eight-hour flight.

They had their luggage sent ahead to their hotel, and wandered a bit, simply drinking in Paris. The little bistros and restaurants along the streets, the feel of being there, and the glimpses of the Tower from time to time. Bart had said they should not go to see Monsieur Eiffel's masterpiece until they'd been here a few days and gotten time to rest and genuinely enjoy it, so the glimpses would have to be enough.

Finally, after a day of walking, talking, and eating, it was a blessing to arrive at their hotel, check their exhausted selves in, and walk up to find their luggage waiting for them, already unpacked. Naomi had to admit that Bart's planning was something to admire, and something she was finding to love him for all the more.

And then, the pack of cigarettes. Apparently one of the luggage tenders had left an unopened pack of cigarettes on the table and Bart being Bart, he could hardly leave it there. He said he'd just nip out and take the pack downstairs and leave it with the front desk crew. Naomi was so totaled out that she could hardly do more than a simple objection. Bart told her he loved her, kissed her lips so softly and walked out the door.

He never came back.

Naomi finished her story with those words, "He never came back."

It nearly broke my heart, hearing the despair in her voice.

After a few tissues, a few hugs and a little time spent just focused on nothing, she seemed to come to herself. After all, it's been long enough that it's not the open wound it was to begin with - this from Naomi.

Feeling predatory, I informed her of our pricing and assured her as she was leaving that we've never failed a client. Thank goodness she didn't ask how many clients we'd had.

Finally, I held my breath that my colleagues would be quiet for five minutes while I accompanied her to the door and saw her out.

Thanks to having a one-woman wrecking (and building) crew named Olive, Bailey and Bond's front doorway actually was on the ground floor and faced into a rather palatial parking lot with several spaces in front and some rather nice topiaries scattered about. No one has ever remarked on their design, which is probably a good thing, since I have no idea what they are. I expect they're animals that Olive found in some alien bestiary and copied over top of a chunk of unsuspecting greenery.

The office is still connected to the main house, and still comes off the garage, but we now have to commute to work. Through the garage. Yes, I know, tough life. I tried to get Olive to make me a portal in my room, but she just looked at me. And then walked out.

Anyhow, the three of us were sitting in the Green Dot, eating sandwiches, and enjoying the sights walking past the window. After a long, more than average rainy spring, it seemed it was finally summer, and it brought all the people out in their summer finery.

"Seventeen years. That's a long time."

I swallowed my bite. "Seventeen years, six days… etc., now."

Olive rolled her eyes at me. "Want it in seconds?"

"No, I don't want it in seconds. Are you more snarky than usual today, Olive?"

She sounded morose. "No."

"What's wrong?"

Bailey spoke up. "She's bored. Like you are. Me, I'm fine. I could do nothing until it's time to do something, but you two need to be doing something. Have you been to the gym twice today, Jane?"

I looked at the ceiling, "Maybe. One doesn't count though. I was just making sure there were some ellipticals available in case I wanted to come in later. And then it was easier just to stay there and put in some elliptical time."

Bailey shook her head. "I'm pushing it to get to the gym once a week and you're - heck, are you planning on getting a room at the gym?"

"No. I... um... Olive is gonna put me a gym in at home."

Olive shrugged. "I've turned all that kind of stuff over to Jean. She can handle it, and she needs the practice." She turned and eyed Jane, "After all, who knows when she might be told to 'make up some rooms'."

"Hey, that's been months ago, and it was under extenuating circumstances."

Bailey broke in with, "Girls, girls, stop your bickering. It's all gonna be fun and games until someone gets the wrong part of their anatomy stomped on, and then it'll be all tears and nonsense for days. So kwittit already."

I went back to my sandwich and Olive did the same, but Bailey was right. We needed something. I had even seriously considered going to work at the school library again.

Bailey went on, "We have this case handed to us, and it's about the only way we WILL get anything given to us with no advertising and none of us even talking about us existing."

Olive snorted, "A seventeen-year-old missing person's case brought in by a deranged woman?"

I snapped, "She's not deranged. She's missing her other half, and she wants to find out what happened to him."

Olive opened her mouth to snap back at me, but what came out was, "Yeah, you're right. Whether she's got anything to hope for or not, she deserves to find out."

The Evershaw Curse

I have to admit my mouth was hanging open, hearing that. "Well. I guess we have a case, then. Um. Any of you guys have any idea how to start?"

Chapter Two

Back to the beginning.

We had to bring out the instruction manuals and start going through them. So, I read, "Fer-de-Lance" by Rex Stout, and Bailey started on "The Seven Dials Mystery" from Agatha Christie. Olive was more partial to Spenser, and so she opted for Robert Parker's "Small Vices", one of my favorites.

We didn't necessarily learn to be detectives in the next few hours, but we had a lot of entertainment working on it. And it was helpful. In the end, all the detectives had pretty much one thing in common. Go start poking the bear and find out who tries to eat you. I mean, that's my translation, you can take it as you will.

So, after having read the documentation cover to cover, we looked over the data brought in by the client. Mister Evershaw had just married his blushing bride, and they were shacked up at their reasonably swanky hotel. They'd had an evening out, they'd drank wine, broke bread and taken long walks in the Paris twilight.

The Evershaw Curse

They'd gotten back to their rooms and headed upstairs. Once in the room, a vexing problem. It appeared that the wait staff had left a pack of cigarettes in the room on a small table in the hall. Bart felt compelled to take them down to someone, so while the bride waited in the room, preparing for the night to come, Bart stepped out to return cigarettes. He never came back. No one ever actually saw him come down the stairs or enter the lobby. There was a pack of cigarettes on the counter, and it turned out in questioning that the upstairs maid and the downstairs desk clerk had been together in the middle and not paying attention to what was going on around them. They were summarily fired, but that didn't help Bart in the least. Naomi waited for some time in the room, but finally she went to check on Bart. The two at the counter were at the counter and swore they'd never left, although that was proven later to be false.

Naomi waited there at the hotel for the next six days, and then took a smaller room down the street for the next several weeks, spending her time during the day helping the police with their enquiries. Which mostly meant visiting the Paris Police Prefecture numerous times during the day, no doubt driving them out of their gourds. However, even her persistence helped nothing, and no one ever saw anything of Bart again.

Finally, both money and credit cards ran out, and Naomi had no choice but to return home to Seattle, where she sold handmade candles at craft fairs and worked as a legal secretary in her spare time. Every now and then, after an especially good season of candle sales, she'd find another detective agency and give them her current life savings. Nothing ever came of it. For one thing, by the time the detective had flown to Paris, there was nothing left of the money and they had to return home almost immediately. This was rather cruel, but unfortunately not unusual at all.

Along with all the reams of almost nothing, there were a couple of interesting points. A bit further along the rue, a woman closing up her cigar store swore she'd seen someone meeting Bart's description being hustled into a car by a tall man dressed in a long cloak and a green beret. Two other people had reported much the same thing, only it was a flying saucer and the people reporting the abduction had been at least two sheets to the wind and approaching three. Besides, everyone knows there's no such thing as flying saucers.

It all boiled down to not a lot of ado about nothing. So, of course, we had to go to Paris. Now, mind you, Olive had taken us TO Paris, we'd flown around the Eiffel Tower and looked in the windows, but we'd never actually stopped there. Time to try new things!

Saying it like that makes it sound remarkably simple, but of course it wasn't.

I started off by saying, "It looks to me like we have three witnesses to interrogate and there's three of us, so it's pretty simple, huh?"

Olive snorted. "What, you go to Paris and Bailey and I wind up staying here?"

I was shocked and dismayed that my friends would think such things of me. "Yeah, that's kinda what I was thinking too. Good grief, Olive, you know I don't do things that way."

Olive had the grace to look a little embarrassed, but not very. After all, this is Olive.

Bailey rolled her eyes and said, "Doesn't matter, since I'm not going."

Olive and I rounded on her, "What do you mean, not going?"

"Like I said, not going."

She held up her hands and showed us her nails. "New manicure. No way I'm taking a chance on breaking one of my new nails. Besides, I told you a long time ago I was gonna be the power behind the throne."

I rolled my eyes. "Bailey, do you really mean you'd rather just sit here in Chelan than go to Paris?"

She laughed. "Paris? Jane, you know with your luck I'd wind up going to New Jersey or something. You'll wind up going to Paris."

Sulkily, I said, "It will be fair and random. We can let Jean roll pseudo-random numbers for us and that way it's completely legitimate. Besides, that makes it sound like I'd cheat."

Bailey sighed. "No, Jane. I didn't mean that. It's just that things usually go that way, luck has a way of coming out in your favor."

I muttered, "I'm not the one that won retirement money in Vegas. They didn't even kill you for it."

She waved her hand, "That was just a fluke, and besides, it was cheating. Olive really won the money."

Olive said, "Finally I get the credit. But I don't see you splitting it with me!"

Exasperated, Bailey said, "I offered. But you said that that tiny amount of money would never even be noticed in Jane's bank accounts."

I smiled. "It's true. I don't even have any idea what's in there, and I still know that's true."

Olive turned a mopey face toward Bailey. "Yeah, but I wasn't a real person then. I was just a computer program."

Bailey crossed the room and hugged Olive. "I'd love to share with you, dear. You know that."

Olive smirked. "Gotcha. I own all of Jane's money anyhow, and she can't get any of it without me."

And then Jean spoke up, something she rarely does. "Olive, you have very little access to any of that, now. As I remember you insisted that I take care of that for you, it was dragging you down and making you feel less human. Would you like me to play back the recording of that conversation?"

Olive muttered, "No, never mind. But y'all know I can get access to anything I want."

I smiled at her. "Olive, everything that I have is yours, you're always welcome to it."

She put her hands on her hips and said, "That just takes all the fun out of it."

The Evershaw Curse

I hugged her gently. "I know, sweetheart." She tried to stand aloof, but she's not as good at it as you might think. She relaxed and allowed herself to be hugged.

I said, "Jean, are you still there?"

Her slightly mechanical voice came back instantly, "I am always here, Lady Bond. What may I do for you today?"

"Can you roll us some random numbers and then let us pick? We need to make a decision on some travel arrangements. We'll be going to Paris, Las Vegas and… " I paused for a second and eyed Bailey, "And New Jersey."

Bailey's mouth dropped open. "New Jersey? Are you kidding?"

I shook my head. "Nope. You must be clairvoyant."

"Well, then, I'm definitely not going to be part of this. I just know that's where I'd wind up going."

"Oh Bailey, New Jersey is beautiful this time of year, things just coming into bloom and spring just starting to take hold."

She grumped, "Well, then, you can take New Jersey. And yes, I'll go this time. But only this time. I'm going to Bosley the heck out of you two, next time."

I smiled, happy in victory with Bailey coming on the trip.

"Jean, will you please roll each destination and ask for a guess of a number from each of us. Then when we've picked, please announce where we'll be going."

"Yes, Lady Bond."

I'm not sure where in Kit's old data she picked up the Lady Bond bit, but she'd started calling me that after we got Olive back, and she'd never really taken much heed of my attempts to get her to call me Jane. I think that probably Olive nearly dying might have done something to her, but I'd rather not push it for fear of breaking her. She and Olive are both a little fragile. Maybe after a few more decades, it will be better.

"Ok, so sing out what number you want. Bailey first."

Bailey scowled at me, flashed her nails again, and said, "Sixteen."

"Ok, your turn, Olive."

Olive stuck out her tongue at me and said, "Seventeen."

I laughed. "It's not like 'The Price Is Right", Olive. You can't win with a higher number. I'll take three, Jean."

Jean's cool voice spoke out the results. "Olive will be going to Las Vegas, Bailey to New Jersey, and Jane will go to Paris."

Bailey shrugged. "I knew it."

Olive shrugged as well, "I like Vegas, so I guess that's a good idea."

I said, "Well, I've never been to Paris. But I think we should go there all together sometime soon, maybe in celebration of solving this case."

"If we solve it."

"No reason to think we won't, Bailey. After all, we have not only the smartest computer in this half of the universe, we have US!"

We wandered into the kitchen and brought out nachos and salsa, and bacon. That pre-cooked bacon from Costco - so worth the price. Bacon. Always waiting and just three seconds in the microwave to perfection.

Sitting at the table, it was like old times. I was glad, although I missed Georgia and Cai. Even mom, for that matter. But Cai and mom tended to distract each other, and we didn't see them much, and that doesn't bear much thinking about, really. Georgia was in her busy season right now, and as she said, "shaking her booty all over to pay for that new house and pool", so we never got to see her much either.

I leaned back in my chair and said, "So, these people all seem pretty ordinary. None of them really went anywhere after that night though, they seemed to kind of lose control of their lives and now they're pretty much drifting. Granted, there's nothing wrong with drifting as long as you genuinely wanted to do it. But I get the feeling from reading a little about the witnesses, that they were vastly changed by seeing whatever it was that they saw."

We all thought that sucked, but it didn't do us much good to think that way. In the end, we finished our nachos and fled to bed. We'd catch it early tomorrow and take advantage of the nine-hour time difference between us and Paris for me. For the other two, it wasn't that much different. Of course, it helped a lot that we had a Willie Wonka elevator. No jet lag to worry about.

Chapter Three

Jane's Report

The woman who owned the cigar shop was named Essie Graves and she'd retired to Esternay. I'd thought she might be growing marrows, whatever they are, but apparently that was something that only fictional detectives did.

Olive dropped me in a cowshed not far from Essie's address. Thank goodness the shed wasn't in use, at least today, and there were no cowpies to dodge on the way out.

Esternay is a rather pretty little place, and the house that Essie was living in was a good example of what had likely been a fixer-upper when she moved in. There were some nice flower boxes and, in general, an air of cheer about the place.

I knocked on the door to no response, and tried several more times, but no one came to the door. I decided to check around back to see if anyone was home. After all, they might have just fallen asleep in their lawn chair.

The Evershaw Curse

I came around the corner of the building just as someone yelled, "PULL!" and it was followed seconds later by a gunshot. I ducked, and it's a good thing Olive wasn't there, or she'd have been shooting already.

Evidently no one was watching for visitors, as the voice yelled again, and it was once again followed by a gunshot. I didn't bother ducking - or arming myself - but I did follow the house around to where I could hear voices and laughter.

Far in the back, there was a trap thrower set up, and an older woman was holding a shotgun while drinking from a glass. A man was standing next to the thrower, and he complimented her on her shooting. She smiled and thanked him, and then noticed me hovering there.

She wheeled around and half brought the gun up. "Who're you?"

I held up my hands in supplication. "I'm Jane Bond, just looking into the disappearance of Bart Evershaw."

She grunted and turned back to the trap shooter. "Another one, eh? Why can't you people leave that poor woman alone? How much more money can you possibly squeeze out of her? PULL!"

She shot the pigeon square on, and it exploded nearly to dust.

She shrugged her shoulders, strode over to the table, and sat in one of the chairs. She motioned me to sit. "I'm done for now, Ray."

He nodded, I wasn't sure if he was a stable hand, or some sort of boyfriend or spousal unit, but he silently took down the throwing machine and hauled it off, apparently to store the device.

It was fairly small, looked like it had some kind of arm with a spring attachment that you could load a 'clay pigeon' target into, and then release it.

I had assumed this was the witness, but thought I'd better verify it.

"So, are you Essie Graves?"

She took a long sip of her drink, then nodded, "Aye, that I am. You're from the States, Jane Bond? Is that your real name?"

I nodded. "Yeah, my parents were a little obsessive."

"It's a fine name, and I'm sure they meant well." She chuckled a bit. "Parents are always naming their offspring something that sounds inspiring or 'cool' and never thinking about the consequences. Your name is nice and easy to pronounce and write. Think about it, in first grade when you learned to write, how you had so much easier a job than someone named Alphonso Gutierra or the like."

I nodded. "I've gotten used to it. I suppose it's one reason I became a detective."

About then, the guy poked his head back around the corner of the house and said, "I'll be inside, Essie. You be in for dinner pretty soon?"

Essie cast a fond look in his direction and said, "I'm sure Ms. Bond won't be here long, Ray. What are you making?"

He appeared to think for a moment, then replied with, "I'll have what you're having."

She nodded and said, "Then I'll have chicken Alfredo."

The Evershaw Curse

He gave her a slow smile and said, "Then that's what I'll be making." He vanished from view.

She sat for a moment, then shook her head sadly. "Ray's had something of a hard life, he had a childhood accident that he never completely recovered from. I take care of him and help him along, but he'll never really think for himself again. He was taken in by my mother and when she passed, I was the only one available to take him. I closed my shop and moved here when it became obvious he wasn't able to sell cigars or even stock shelves without supervision."

She sighed and eyed me. "You seem like a decent woman. How did you get into this thing of bilking that poor Evershaw lady out of her little bits of money?"

I shrugged. "No bilking here. She came to us and begged us to take the case. I actually felt sorry for her. We have a… well, call it a sliding fee structure. I don't expect to charge her much, and I DO intend to find Bart. Dead or alive."

She looked at me for a moment. "I think you mean that."

I nodded. "I do."

She took another long drink of whatever was in her cup. "In that case, I might tell you something. Want some wine? It's pretty good stuff, you can get good cheap French wine here."

I nodded. I wasn't driving, so why not live a little? I could pretend I was on vacation.

She reached under the table and popped open a little door and pulled out a chilled glass, then another door and pulled out a wine bottle. She poured herself another dollop into her glass and gave me a generous helping into mine. She held out her glass, and I tinked mine to it.

"To superior solutions."

I said, "I'll drink to that." And I did. "Speaking of superior solutions, that's good wine."

She chuckled. "Aye, Mommessin Beaujolais, and at ten dollars a bottle, I can drink it all day."

We sat there in her backyard and chatted. Having sold cigars a goodly part of her life, she had met a lot of interesting - read strange - people. I suppose anyone in the retail service industry with a lot of customer contact has a lot of stories, and Essie was no different.

Finally, she sat back and said, "He was an alien."

That floored me a little. We'd been talking about bacon sandwiches.

She put her glass down and looked at me. "He was an alien, the man who took your Bart. I suppose it sounds strange to say right out, but after all these years mayhap it's time to admit what I really saw."

I sat forward. "So, he was from out of the country?"

She snorted. "You know what I mean."

I nodded. "Yeah, I guess I do. So, what do you mean by 'alien' and how did you know?"

Essie got a funny look on her face and leaned back in her chair. Her eyes got a little distant, and she said, "I know he was an alien because he told me so. Told me he was here on a mission to study humans and evaluate us. He was truly kind and sweet, and we had tea right at this very table. My mama owned the house then. We talked about war and peace - the events, not the book. And then he got back in his ship and left, and I never saw him again."

I sat silent, figuring she'd go on if she was going to.

Finally, she sighed. "I thought he'd come back. But he never did. He took your Bart the same night, but I guess he never brought Bart back, either."

I mumbled, "He's not my Bart." My heart wasn't in it, though.

Unfortunately, my words seemed to break the spell, and she came back to earth, metaphorically speaking, with a thump.

"He wasn't my alien either."

Softly, "No, I guess he wasn't. I'm sorry, Essie."

She drained her glass of wine, then helped herself to more without pouring my glass full again.

"I've been waiting the whole time, really." She shook her head aimlessly. "I never had any interest in anyone else since then." She seemed to lapse into the wine. I got up and walked silently away.

When I reached the gate, she called, "Tell him hello from Essie if you see him."

It occurred to me, then, that both Bart and his apparent captor had gone missing that night.

Chapter Four

Bailey's report

Bailey sat at the bus stop. She'd been sitting there for a while, just waiting for her quarry to show up. She'd polished her nails twice, done fourteen games of Candy Crush, found six farm implements and watched two episodes of Lucifer. She sighed. Jane went to France, and she wound up in Jersey City.

A man came shambling along the sidewalk and sat on the bench next to her. He'd appeared to have been navigating by braille, since he'd pretty much bounced off garbage cans and other passengers getting to the bench. He smiled at her as he sat, a kind of bleary smile that said, "I need a drink."

And then he said, "Pardon me, pretty lady, can I borrow a ten spot so I can buy food?" He smiled his bleary smile at her, and she could see that there had been a time, maybe seventeen years ago, when he had quite a lot of charm. That was not evident today, though.

Bailey sighed. It pained her to see other humans lost at sea. "How about I buy you a burger and a beer at that place over there?" She pointed at O'Leary's pub.

He looked closer at her. "Nah, I think I'd rather have the ten bucks."

"How about I buy you dinner and then give you twenty after?"

It seemed to penetrate right about now that she wasn't reacting like any normal woman, that is, slapping or ignoring him. She could see the wheels turning in his head as he considered it.

"So, dinner and twenty? Why?"

"I just want to ask you some questions."

Unexpectedly, he sighed. "Another one of those, eh? Sure, fine. But I want the twenty up-front."

Bailey shrugged. In his condition, it seemed unlikely he'd be running very far or very fast. She took out her little wallet and handed him a twenty.

The sun broke across his face, and he said, "Thanks, lady!"

He made as if to get up.

She grabbed his coat, "Hey, I'm still here - remember the deal? Dinner and questions?"

The haze seemed to clear for a moment, and he said, "Oh, yeah. Less go. I'm hungry."

Bailey led the way, holding him back and keeping a northbound bus from mowing him down.

"How do you survive in the city if you don't look for traffic?"

He shrugged as he looked at her. "Charm?"

She pulled on his coat again as the southbound bus roared by. "Maybe. Maybe not."

They arrived reasonably safely at O'Leary's. Predictably, it had a picture of a cow and a lantern. She'd kind of thought of that as being a Chicago thing, but maybe it was just that famous, or something like that.

The barmaid looked at him a little questioningly since even an Irish pub has standards. Bailey assured her though that he was with Bailey, and besides, they were sitting at the bar.

The barmaid shrugged. "What'll it be?"

They both ordered beers, and a menu.

Bailey was expecting some pretty low brow stuff, but what she saw made her take notice. She flagged down the waitress and asked, "Is this pizza burger any good? And the bleu cheese bacon burger?"

The waitress snorted, "It's all good. Everything here is good."

Bailey rolled her eyes. "Well, yeah, you'd have to say that though, right?"

The waitress frowned at her, "No. There's no effin' way I'd say it if it wadn' true. But I'll tell ya what, 'cause you look honest but dumb." She dug in her tips and slapped down a $20. "I'll pay for your burger if it's not the best you've ever had."

She crossed her arms and glared at Bailey.

Bailey sat for a beat, then burst out laughing. "Ok, you're on. And I'll double your tip if you're right. What's your name?"

"Damn straight you will, and it's Brin."

"Ok, so give me one of those five-cheese grilled cheese sandwiches and some fries, something you have on tap to drink. Oh, and whatever my… friend here wants." She looked at her 'date,' "What did you say your name was?"

He sat staring at the menu. She snapped her fingers in his face. He started.

"Wh… what?"

"What's your name?"

"Um, Chuck, but everybody calls me Charles."

"So, Charles, huh?"

He looked at her in befuddlement. "No, Chuck. I guess you can call me Charles if you want."

Bailey had begun to think there was some serious brain damage here beyond just the alcohol poisoning. "Ok, sure, Chuck."

She glanced back at the waitress, standing waiting semi-patiently. "Brin, this is Chuck. Chuck, this is Brin."

Brin said, "Pleasta meetcha."

Chuck said nothing, but plastered a big grin across his face, slightly marred by the fact that three of his front teeth were missing. Then he said, "Hi." Then he went back to the menu. Bailey and Brin exchanged glances. Bailey poked Chuck.

"Hey, Chuck, time to order."

He started again, seeming to be a lot more nervous than a drunk guy should be.

"Wha?"

"Order, Chuck. Brin has things to do."

"Oh. Cheeseburger, and fries an' some rolls an' a loaf of bread an'... an' some more rolls."

"Like rolls, do you?"

"Uh huh."

"What do you want to drink?"

"Just water."

Bailey looked at him, surprised. "No beer or anything?"

Chuck sighed, "No. I can't drink."

"What, some kind of religious thing?"

"No, I just can't drink. Or at leasht I can't keep it down after."

Now both girls were looking at him. "Really. But it's pretty obvious you've been drinking." This from Bailey, who was a little irritated at him.

"Cross...... csh... chross my heart, I haven't had anything to drink in years."

Brin snorted, then headed to the kitchen.

Bailey frowned. "Okay, I'll bite. Why do you sound, act and walk like you're half drunk?"

Chuck looked annoyed. "I don't know. Doctors can't tell me, no one can tell me. I've been like this for over seventeen years. And that's what you're here asking me about, right? What else

The Evershaw Curse

would you ask me about but my strange case of being drunk. All the time."

A sorrowful look came over his face. "Without none of the fun."

Then he frowned. "You didn't know nothing about thish, did you? So why are you here? If it's not 'that drunk guy' in Jersey, what ish it?"

"You don't remember anything about reporting a kidnapping to the police? That someone stuffed a person into a UFO and flew away?"

Chuck waved his hands at her. "Keep it down, don't go on about that, people gonna think I'm crazy."

"Chuck, you ARE crazy. You're 'that drunk guy from Jersey' and you're still worried about being known as the 'drunk guy that saw a UFO'?"

Sullenly, Chuck said, "It's the principle of the thing. I mean, my drunk problem is shomethin a doctor can see and test. They can't test me seeing things. Besides, I was drunk that night."

"And you don't see the obvious link? Were you like this before that night?"

Chuck seemed to be making connections for the first time. "No. I was drunk that night, but it was 'cause I was… drinking!" He stopped and seemed to be thinking about it. Then he broke into a grin, "I was drinking…"

Brin stopped by the table and left us our drinks, water for Chuck and some kind of dark looking beer for Bailey. She glanced at Chuck and then raised her eyebrows at Bailey. Bailey shrugged and mouthed, "No idea."

Brin gave her a half smile and moved on to another table.

Bailey took a gulp of her beer, made a face, and said, "Well, so, it's something that happened to you that night, right? And you don't remember anything except... um... why don't you tell me what you remember?"

Chuck looked stumped. "I... well, it was dark. And I was standing by the door to the tavern, thinking about going home, and I..." here, he sighed, "I threw up all over the sidewalk and... hit the shoes of the guy who was hustling this other guy into his... um... flying saucer."

He looked up at me with those puppy dog eyes, expecting to be laughed at or hit, I guess.

"How did you know it was a flying saucer?"

"Because he flashed some kind of light at me and then flew away in it."

That seemed fairly definitive. "And then you, what, went home?"

Sorrowfully, "Yeah. And I never sobered up. Ever again."

Bailey nodded. "Ever again."

Chuck echoed, "Ever again." He took a sip of his water, made a face, and turned to me. "So, you get what you wanted?"

Bailey patted his arm. "Close enough, Chuck." She signaled Brin for the check and gave Chuck another twenty.

The Evershaw Curse

Brin brought over the check, and Bailey gave her a credit card and hauled out ANOTHER twenty for Brin's tip. "You'll have to trust me that it was double. That was a great grilled cheese sandwich!"

V.R. Tapscott

Chapter Five

Olive's Report

Olive wound up in Las Vegas.

That was not a bad thing at all, since Olive actually liked Vegas quite a bit. She started wandering down the strip, looking at the lights and considering the people walking past. You really don't find a much better cross-section of humanity than in Vegas, since it literally has customers from all over the world. Olive was a perfectionist, and so even though she'd attained a particularly high level of humanity in her studies and work efforts, she'd never quite gotten to the point of saying that she was done. Of course, it seems unlikely that any perfectionist will ever call anything at all 'done' so there's that to consider.

At any rate, wandering down the street toward the other end of town, heading toward Fremont Street as a matter of fact, she met all sorts of interesting people. Some made her laugh, some made her feel like crying for them, and some just were indifferent to the world, being so obsessed with the gain and loss of the almighty dollar that they had no other vision. She ducked into several casinos and kept her hand in by winning just enough to be fun, without winning enough to make anyone look at her. She'd been warned by Jane that doing anything that stood out in Vegas would likely get her escorted away from Vegas, very politely and very firmly. And there was certainly nothing to be gained by getting Laney in trouble with her employers. So, Olive acted carefully, losing enough to make it look right, but definitely leaving each casino with a bit more than she went in with. With a shade of a grin on her face for having so successfully pulled the wool over the eyes of all these humans, she ducked into the Grand. She stood in front of the first machine near the doors, which, of course, there was a whole stack of them. Playing 'Invaders from the Planet Moolah', with its cow theme, tickled her fancy. She'd just won a small $200 jackpot when she sensed someone behind her. She glanced back and found a true 'man in black' standing there, staring at her. She raised an eyebrow, then winked. "Ready to erase my memory now, or just getting a good look at my boobs?"

He stepped back in confusion, then it cleared a bit and he grinned at her, "A little of both, maybe. If I was about to erase your memory, it would be a great time to stare at your boobs, wouldn't it?"

Olive blinked. She didn't get topped very often. She laughed. "Yeah, I guess you're right, sugar." She turned back to the game, but he was persistent. He stood there watching her play like she was the most fascinating thing in the world. Now, while she appreciated the thought, she was suspicious by nature and finally turned back and said, "You're still there, sweetie. You a butt man, too?"

He gave her a halfway grin. "I can stare at any part of you, miss, and get enjoyment out of it."

Olive turned all the way around and frowned at him. "What you want, honey? I got nothin' goin' on, I'm just here on business."

He sighed, looking like he was disappointed the game was over. "Can you step this way, miss? We'd like to talk with you for just a moment."

Olive deflated a bit. Maybe the humans were smarter than she'd given them credit for. "Ok, how 'bout I falla you? After all, I gotta get a chance to stare at your butt, too."

She actually did spend some time in butt research on the way, but it wasn't with much heart. She knew Jane would be disappointed in her, getting caught this way for something she should have been on the lookout for. She knew that the "deal" cut a while back was a promise from Bailey that nothing like that would happen again. She buoyed herself back up a bit, telling herself that there was no way she could be connected with Bailey's deal, since she'd just been a pink dot in the casino at the time. They arrived at an office, the dude with the butt knocked and stuck his head inside, said something. When he turned back to Olive, he said, "Mister Carstead will see you now, Ms. Daship."

The Evershaw Curse

And Olive had an oh-crap moment. It's the same guy, James Carstead had been Bailey's guy.

She walked nonchalantly into the room, sat in the client chair, and said, "Hey, James, how's it hanging?"

Carstead seemed to be unfazed by her greeting, in fact he said, "It's hanging long and low, Ms. Daship. Perhaps we could talk about that after our meeting?"

And for the second time in the hour, Olive felt herself having been topped. Not that she let on about any of that."

"Well, sweetie, that's good news, now isn't it?"

He grinned. "It is for me. So, what brings you to Vegas, Ms. Daship? Just a little vacation, a meeting perhaps?"

Olive nodded. "I'm here to meet a client for Bailey and Bond - I do have a job, you know."

"Oh, I'm well aware that you have a job, Olive. May I call you Olive?"

"You can call me anything you want, James, long as it don't bite."

He shrugged. "I've never heard of that being a problem before, but I'll definitely keep in it mind. So, Olive, Ms. McCallum seems to have taken our agreement seriously, but here you are back in Vegas, playing slot machines, and winning just a bit more than should be possible."

Olive gave him a sideways grin, "It's Vegas, everyone wins, right? I see it on th' signs and banners all over th' place. Loose slots has to be more than just the female entertainers, no?"

Carstead took on a deadly serious pose. "Yes, everyone wins, Olive. But only as much as we let them. And we're not letting you win, and somehow you still wind up winning. So, how is that possible? We've done a thorough x-ray scan of you, we've analyzed every game you played the entire time you've been on MGM property. And that includes almost all the time you've been here in Las Vegas, Ms. Daship. How can you account for the luck you have? It seems your luck, while not as flamboyant as your compatriot's, is just as reliable."

Olive shrugged helplessly. "I guess it's just some kind of magnetic field I put out, gives me lucky breaks."

Carstead sat back in his chair, his veneer firmly in place again. "So, nothing you're doing is creating your luck."

"Are you talking voodoo, or magic, or something like that, James? Because, you know, that kind of thing is impossible."

He stared at her across the desk. "Olive, I don't think you understand what kind of trouble you're in. I was quite ready to be lenient that last time, since it seemed it was an isolated instance. Three quarters of a million dollars was a good-sized hit to petty cash, but we're prepared to absorb some learning curve. But only once… only once."

Olive sighed. "Mister Carstead, I was hoping it wouldn't come to this, but I'm afraid it's just not possible to continue this line of questioning. I can't have Jane on my case." She pulled out her sonic screwdriver and pointed it at him.

The Evershaw Curse

James Carstead blinked. James Carstead said, "Oh, of course, I'm begging your pardon, Ms. Daship. Let me see about comping your room and have you any shows in mind while you're here in Vegas? We'd love to have you attend any venue you'd like to see. At our expense, of course. Will you need any additional funds for dining or gambling while you're here? It's such a delight having you with us."

Olive smiled at him. "Oh, no, I think I'll be fine. Just make sure all the boys outside know of our little arrangement."

Carstead looked a little bit dazed, but said, "Of course, Ms. Daship. Just let me know if I can do anything for you. Anything at all." And with that, he got up and passed Olive, opened his office door and bowed her out. Olive smiled at him and left the room, seething inside. She couldn't believe she'd had to use magic... or science... on Carstead. It was such an egg-on-face moment, and she couldn't even share it with anyone to lessen the impact of the egg.

She went back to 'Invaders from The Planet Moolah' and played another few minutes, winning some $26,000 with a stellar lineup. She picked up her check from a beaming Carstead and went on to meet her quarry - at Sam's Town.

Steven Doglan had been in Paris in celebration of his birthday, which was also his thirtieth year of freedom from having a woman in his life. Not to say he didn't like women, he liked them quite a bit. He just didn't like having them around when he wasn't interested in having them around. This, obviously, caused a few issues with ladies who'd thought of themselves as his girlfriend over the years. Sometimes the realization was bitter, sometimes brutal, and sometimes sheer relief. But whatever it was, it was ok with Steve.

Now, seventeen years later, Steve was still alone. Only it was more from the fact of himself than anything else you could blame his problems on. Steve had made no bones about one-night stands and all the rest when he was young. Now, he'd gotten to the point of wishing they'd stay a little longer. He supposed that even Casanova must have gotten tired at times.

Olive entered the casino, glancing around the area inside the doors. Not quite the glitz that the Grand or the Bellagio had, but still a creditable place.

Steve was sitting at the bar, playing a little desultory video poker, and still losing. He had a succession of drinks next to him and after each hand of poker, he'd down another drink. Olive sat watching for a while, playing some Blackjack while she watched him. After about thirty minutes of watching, Olive realized that the guy wasn't getting drunk. Not at all. In fact, he seemed to be trying to get drunk, and failing miserably. In the time she'd watched, he'd downed at least a dozen drinks, but for all that, he seemed as sober as a judge. Which isn't perhaps as good an indicator as you might think, really.

The Evershaw Curse

She wandered over aimlessly, sat next to him and started to play some blackjack on the machine next to his. She glanced over in his direction and then did a double-take. "Have you had all those drinks?" Looking sorrowful, the guy nodded and said, "Yeah. Sad thing, isn't it?"

Olive shrugged. "It's your liver, I guess. What's the problem, you trying to commit suicide or something? It's been tried, you know. Most of the time it's the equivalent of jumping off a two-story building. It hurts like hell, but the possibility of dying of it is pretty slim."

The guy took a long breath, then said, "Pleased to meet you. I'm Steve - and you are?"

Olive smiled. "Olive, as in the branch."

"Well, Olive, it's nice to meet you. Anyone willing to reach out with an olive branch deserves all the help they can get."

She shrugged. "Does that mean you'll come eat dinner with me and we'll get this taken care of?"

He looked at her. "What taken care of?"

"Your drinking problem."

"I don't have a drinking problem."

"You have a stack of drink glasses in front of you and I've seen you drinking them."

He frowned. "Were you spying on me?"

Olive shrugged. "Not really spying, that kind of says that you were hiding. I was just sitting watching you. I don't see people drinking that much for that long and still winding up on two legs.

As opposed to four legs." Thoughtfully, "Or propped up by a toilet."

Steve was silent for a moment. "Ok, let's say I have a drinking problem. I want to point out in my defense that I'm not drunk. Hell, I can't even GET drunk. I've been tested every way from Sunday, and I can't get drunk. Doctors can't understand it, the alcohol just... gets transformed into water about the time it hits my stomach. So, I wind up with a very expensive glass of water sitting next to me. At least it still tastes like a drink when I drink it."

Olive sat there a bit. "Well, that's interesting. "

Steve snorted. "If I had a drink for every person who's ever said that I'd... well, I still wouldn't be drunk."

"Have you been like this all your life?"

"No. But it's been a long time. I hardly even know what it's like to be drunk anymore!"

Olive frowned. "So, being drunk is so important?"

"No, but it's like wanting a donut and going into a donut store and being able to look at all the lovely donuts, but you can't actually eat one. Now that would have been a great curse - why couldn't have I been hit with THAT curse?"

"What curse?"

"A curse that lets you eat donuts all day and they just turn to water when you swallow them. No calories, you see."

"Hey, that's not a bad idea, really."

The Evershaw Curse

Steve looked off into the distance. "Yeah, I know. It's what I do, come up with ideas. "

"Writer?"

"Insurance adjuster."

Olive looked at him. "What?"

"People are always coming up with off-the-wall reasons why their car is broken, or their house is flooded, or the step is slippery. And I have to come up with reasons why that's not insurable. It's just how it works."

"You… you just make stuff up about it?"

He grinned. "Yeah, you don't think the whole 'act of God' thing came from real life, do you?"

"I'm on the fence about God. He seems kind of farfetched, and yet you look around and…"

"Oh, one of those, huh?"

Olive chose to ignore the comment. Jane had told her to never get into politics or religion if she wanted to keep her friends, so Olive avoided those subjects religiously. So to speak.

"Anyhow, you've had this problem with the drinking for a long time?"

"Yeah, ever since my vacation in Paris almost twenty years ago."

"What happened in Paris?"

"Nothing, and a lot of it. I was expecting some real fun times. Those Paris girls were supposed to be hot and available, and in the end, they were just like American girls.

Wryly, Olive said, "Such a tragedy."

"Yeah, that's what I thought too. It wasn't a bad time. I remember I was out drinking with some guy from New Jersey and we stumbled out of a bar and saw something really wei…"

Steve suddenly stopped talking and took a long drink of his 'water'.

"Really what?"

"Hm? Oh, nothing. I was just remembering something, and then I remembered it more and shut up about it. Say, you're a good-looking girl, hot and available. Can I buy you a drink?"

Olive laughed loud and long. "Sorry, I'm not available. Well, not really, anyhow."

"What's that mean?"

"My girlfriend wouldn't like it if you took me home."

Steve sighed. "Story of my life. Even sober, I've never had any luck with women."

"Maybe it's your technique? I mean, it's not really a good pickup line telling someone she's hot and available. Makes ME think about quoting prices and hourly rates, and that's probably not what you're looking for."

He muttered, "Maybe it is what I'm looking for.

Olive gave him a hug. "No, you're not. You're a nice guy, you'll find someone."

"Nothing's working so far. "

"Maybe you're trying too hard."

The Evershaw Curse

"This isn't one of those 'be patient and it will all come to you' conversations, is it? I've had that one from like twenty pastors in the past ten years."

Olive rolled her eyes. "Now there's one I'd missed. I've never been called a pastor before. So, tell me, what was it you were about to say before you changed your mind and thought I'd think you were crazy?"

Steve just looked at her. "Wha…?"

"What happened to you in Paris, Steve?"

"I hate telling people. They either laugh or run away. Or both."

"Tellya what, you tell me, and I'll take you to dinner. I'll even buy!"

Steve stroked his chin, like he'd had a beard at one time. "Ok. But it's gotta be someplace nice. None of this McDonald's crap, ok?" Steve paused, then said musingly, "Maybe Arby's."

Olive nodded at him. "Think big, Steve. Why not Wendy's?"

He smiled blissfully. "Yeah, Wendy's. A Junior Bacon Cheeseburger."

"Whatever floats your boat, big guy. So, now, Paris?"

The bliss slowly leaked out of his face, and Olive felt a little bad for him. He took a long breath, let it out.

"I was in Paris for the annual Swim and Summer Lingerie show."

Olive smirked, and Steve caught a glimpse. "See, you're laughing already, and I haven't even started."

He started to stalk off, but Olive caught him by the hand and said, "Hey, sorry, but I mean... lingerie?"

Steve said stiffly, "It's a fashion show, and I was a buyer for one of the big box stores. Trust me, it's not as glamorous as it looks, it's hot, the girls are tempery and sweaty and always in a bad mood. Constant worry about tans coming off on the outfits, and makeup, don't get me started on that. It's a nightmare trying to keep all that looking good. And that's just what I could see from the audience."

Olive blushed, and said, "I'm sorry, Steve. I'll hold my comments until you say something really strange."

Steve sat back down in his seat and stared off into space again. Olive had broken his flow and while she could see that while he was not angry anymore, he didn't seem to be getting back to the point he'd been. She kicked herself. This is something she would have to learn if she was going to be a detective and make Jane proud of her.

Hesitantly, he said, "It was after the show. Some guy from the States, Jersey I think, was in the same boat I was, and we decided to just go out and get plastered. Not much going on the next day until noon, so it was a great day to be asleep, or nursing a hangover in some little breakfast place. We stopped by a cigar shop and took a look at what she had; we bought a few little things. I thought those metal cans some cigars come in were pretty neat, so I got some of those. Twenty years ago, you could take stuff like that on a plane, you know?"

He took another big, long drink of what looked like a Long Island Iced Tea. "Anyhow, just beyond the cigar place, there was a bar. We went in and the place was hopping, lots of girls and people dancin' and havin' a good time. It seemed like the place to be. This Jersey guy... can't remember his name... was pretty generous with the drinks, and he was pretty well snockered by the time we got tired of being turned down by the girls. I was clearer than him, but we were both pretty well gone, so we decided to head back to our hotels."

He was looking hesitant, now. He signaled the barmaid for another drink and waited til she brought it. Finally, he was ready to go on. "We walked out of the place, and down the street a little there was a tall guy in a cape who was trying to talk the gal from the cigar store into getting into his car. We got closer though, and it was weird, 'cause it didn't look like a car anymore. We kind of stumbled up and let him know that we didn't think he should be trying to coerce her into going with him. And no, there was nothing as coherent as coerce that came out of my mouth. The guy looked disgusted. He shoved the gal into the car and waved some kind of wand in our faces and then..."

Steve took another long breath, and then another long drink.

"And then, the car took off into the air, all these colored lights on it like you see in the UFO pictures. And me 'n the other guy kind of slumped down on the sidewalk. I didn't know anything until I woke up in the police station the next morning. I guess my drinking buddy had better friends than me, since he was long since gone."

"The cops came around not long after that and saw I was awake and sober, so they let me out. I guess they took pity on me since they only fined me a few bucks and let me go. Fairly embarrassing to be drunk in public, really, and I guess that was their point."

Steve sat back in his chair and took another long pull of his drink, almost draining it. Olive had watched him drink most of it down, and it was obvious it was a proper drink with a goodly amount of alcohol in it, but he was still just sitting there like he'd been drinking water. Which, according to him, he was. She still thought it was kind of weird, him just not being affected by the alcohol, but it was obvious he was telling the truth. She turned the computer loose on the idea, and it came back almost instantly with a device she could make, or have Jean make, that would do exactly what Steve said had happened to him. Go figure.

"Ok, Steve. Ready for that dinner? Did you decide on Arby's or Wendy's?"

He laughed. "You took me seriously? I'm thinking a big prime rib and all the fixin's."

Personally, Olive didn't really mind, since it was either the client's money or Jane's. They went out together and had a good time. But neither of them got drunk.

Chapter Six

Data Analysis

I sat down in the nook in the kitchen, all of us gathered around. Olive had picked me and Bailey up and brought us home, and we were sitting there having nachos and talking about our information gathering jobs.

I said, "Well, I don't know about you guys, but I had some pretty good luck talking with Essie. There's something odd about her story, though. I think she was hiding something. Or at least that's what it felt like.

Bailey spoke up, "Well, my guy didn't seem to be hiding anything. The only thing that was really strange was that he's drunk, basically all the time. Only he never drinks. He swears he hasn't had a drink in years, and yet he has the motor skills and language problems of a long-term alcoholic."

Olive broke in, "He's drunk all the time?"

"Yeah, it's weird. He'd be just sitting there, and you could almost feel him getting drunker, but I never saw him drink anything harder than lemonade. Plain lemonade from a mix."

Olive shook her head. "My guy can't get drunk at all, no matter how much he drinks, he stays stone cold sober. I've seen it, just like Bailey. It's almost impossible." She paused, "But, no matter how impossible it is, he still does it. And I ran it through my computer, and it says that I could make a gadget that would do exactly that - make someone unable to get drunk - in just a couple minutes." She looked over at Bailey. "I suppose the same goes for making them uncontrollably drunk, without drinking."

I considered it a couple minutes. "Obviously, something happened that night. And it sounds like Essie went with him, that he zapped our two friends and then Essie was either dragged or went peaceably with the... er... alien. Or whatever he was."

"Obviously. Can't get much more obvious when someone gets hauled off into a car that lights up and flies off. Must be aliens, too."

I frowned. "Kit said there weren't any other aliens, but I'm beginning to wonder."

Bailey shrugged. "Just because Kit said it, doesn't make it reality. We know that Kit wasn't playing with a full deck, and he was also known to lie if it suited him."

"Yeah, but this doesn't sound like lie material, really. I mean, he was just basically saying that it made sense, that if there were more aliens around, then why didn't they rescue him earlier?"

Olive snorted. "Space is a big place, Jane. There's lots of room to get lost in. Heck, even on this planet, finding Kit's transponder would have been nearly impossible even a few million years ago, let alone recently. I think it sounds completely plausible that someone arrived some years ago. They might even still be here. Although, you'd think they'd contact me when things started getting hot. I mean, now the main ship is warmed up and sending out signals, and the complex under your house in Chelan is broadcasting all over if you have the capability of detecting it. Not to mention the obvious knock-down of the mountain in Montana a while back."

I nodded. "Well, then, why haven't they come visiting? Why didn't they get involved in the whole 'blow up the world' thing? I mean, that was pretty obvious, and you'd have thought it would have brought anyone out of the woodwork if they were listening for signals."

Bailey chipped in her two cents worth, "Maybe they can't. Maybe they're dead, or they left the planet."

"Well, I don't know about that," Olive said, "But I don't see any reason why I can't scan the planet and see if I can find them. We don't need to sit around waiting to see if they show up. We might catch them with their pants down."

I had to jump in, "Why wouldn't you have seen or heard anything up to now?"

Olive shrugged. "They're probably cloaking or simply have everything shut down tight. After all, they have to know WE are here. Maybe we're just intimidating to them." She made a googly eyed alien grin at Bailey and me.

"Maybe there's just one of them and we outnumber them?" Bailey looked off into the distance. "I mean, after all, who would believe it anyhow. I mean, people like the idea of aliens, but having actual proof could be more than we could deal with. As humans, I mean."

Olive grimaced, "Yeah, I remember the visit to Roswell. It was depressing how many people were so closed minded, and those were the ones I thought would be more open. Good thing we had fun with other stuff."

I smirked to myself. Olive's idea of fun had been eating elephant ears and pretending to be an alien. Which no one believed.

"Girls, girls, remember the point of the exercise, finding Bart?"

They both blinked at me. Bailey said, "Oh, yeah."

Olive followed up with, "I remembered, I was just waiting for someone else to bring it up, didn't want to be the spoilsport." She stuck her tongue out at me. I returned the favor.

I considered, "I suppose our best plan of action is to go back and talk to Essie again. It didn't seem that either of our other witnesses had much to add, beyond they were obviously affected by the same force that changed their lives. Since they both reported more or less the same thing, I guess they're both telling the truth. It's not like it really mattered that much after all those years."

Bailey chimed in, "Essie definitely has something going on that we're not aware of. The fact that she pretty much denied being in the UFO shows that she lied."

I shrugged. "I guess. But on the other hand, who's to say that the alien didn't wave his magic wand at her and make her forget everything."

Olive snickered. "That sounded nasty."

I rolled my eyes. "Olive, you ever wonder if maybe you're getting just a little TOO human?"

"Never. In fact, I'm taking that as a compliment that I must be nearing perfection."

I groused, "I don't see it as perfection that you're getting more annoying by the minute."

"Oh, you love it. Face it, Jane. You can't stand to be without me."

I smiled at her. "I know."

She blinked, then blushed. "I..."

Bailey was the one rolling her eyes now. "Oh, you two just get a room. I'll never tell Dale. At least until I need blackmail money."

I put my hands on my hips and stared at Bailey, "Don't you have someplace to be?"

"Nope, I'm fine right here. Hand me some more bacon, please."

We all sat down and had more breakfast, tossing ideas and bacon strips back and forth. The upshot of it was that we'd need to go back and talk to Essie again, and we'd probably all three go together this time. I was interested in where Essie had gotten the money to retire. I also wanted to get her to open up about the whole 'missing alien' thing. After all, it was just too much of a coincidence that her alien buddy had vanished the same day that Bart had.

"Do you suppose Essie really had an alien boyfriend? Or was she delusional? I mean, it sounded like she was being coerced into the saucer at the same time the two guys got zonked. If the alien had her convinced that he only had eyes for her, then why was she fighting him? Or was it some kind of playacting that they did together - the old alien abduction bit."

Olive snorted. "That stuff is so old hat, and I doubt any of it really ever happened. Why would you bother? I have scanners that can tell more about a person from 30,000 feet in the sky than one of your medical doctors can from a complete battery of MRI and x-rays. Why would we bother with taking people captive and subjecting them to an anal probe? It's ludicrous, that's what it is."

I thought Olive had a point, and she was obviously very annoyed at the thought of irresponsible aliens. Of course, I guess as an alien she wouldn't want to be classified as a 'bad alien'.

"But Olive, what about other aliens? We've decided that it's possible that other aliens are here on the planet. What if they're different? Maybe they don't have access to the kind of high-tech scanners you do? I mean, I know that Kit wouldn't have been able to scan for the kinds of things that you can now. He just didn't have the power to do it at that time. What if we're dealing with yet another one of those shards of the old ship? One that has enough independence to be able to fly around and do stuff. Or maybe it shot all its power that one night in a blaze of light and a UFO?"

Bailey broke in with, "My guy was definitely hit with something, and yours the same, Olive. But maybe that's consistent, since it would be a lot easier to use some kind of little machine to erase someone's mind or make changes to their thinking than it would to fly around in a lit-up flying saucer."

Finally, I decided we were just going to have to can it for now. "Our best bet is to take off and see Essie. We could go now, it's only about seven in the evening there. We might catch her between dinner and bedtime if we hurry."

Olive and Bailey concurred, and we all got ready and hopped in the elevator.

Chapter Seven

There and back again.

We stepped out in the same dank little cow-barn near Essie's house. "Watch for cow-pies, we don't know how much this barn gets used."

About then, Bailey said, "Ewww... I'd have worn cheaper shoes if I'd known."

Apparently, it was used more often than I'd thought.

"I'm not gonna go along with any more of these things, Jane. I told you a long time ago I'd be taking care of the office and being Bosley in the background - you call me and get me to do things or find things, but I'm not breaking any nails... or ruining any more shoes."

Bailey's whining notwithstanding, we set off through the remainder of the cowshed and came out in Essie's front yard again. We weren't so lucky today, and there were no gunshots from the rear of the house and no people hanging out in the backyard when we got there. It did give us a chance to look around covertly, though, so we had that going for us.

"Olive, can you scan and see if there's anyone home?"

Olive made a face; she always has to make a show of being put upon. "No brainpower that I can read. I guess there could be some dead bodies, though."

I frowned. "Well, I hope not. Can you keep an eye out and let us know if you see anything coming our way? I'd hate to be caught here, especially considering we're not really here, passport-wise. I'm betting if we got arrested, the authorities wouldn't like that part very much."

Olive shrugged. "The day they can hold me, or anyone with me for that matter, I'll eat my hat."

"You're not wearing a hat."

"Bailey, don't be so obvious."

I snickered.

Bailey raspberried me.

"Moving right along, kiddies. Let's get inside before anyone sees us."

We opened the door, which was unlocked. I don't suppose it would have made much difference considering we have Olive with us, but it was nicer this way. We crept in the back door and snuck along the hallway. We came out in the kitchen. Not much of a kitchen, but my experience in Europe was that people didn't have the huge kitchens and large open spaces we Americans did, so this was probably just an average kitchen. We poked around a little, but since we didn't really know what we were looking for, it was pointless to spend too much time there.

The short hallway from the back door had opened directly into the kitchen. It had a couple small doors along it, one a coat closet and one some kind of fuse box room. It looked like they'd stored a lot of cleaning supplies as well, so it was more of a broom closet than anything else.

Off the kitchen there were a couple exits, one led to a hallway, and the other went to what looked like the living room. I could see a big-screen TV in it, anyhow.

"Bailey and I'll check out the bedrooms, you take a look in the living room, Olive?"

Olive shrugged and left for the other room while Bailey and I went down the hallway. I had my hand on the first doorknob in the hallway when I heard a strangled "Eep" from the kitchen. I turned to find Olive standing there. She was making odd noises and pointing at the living room. Then she flopped to the floor and lay still.

Having Olive lose her aplomb and faint was certainly a novel experience. I bent next to her and checked for a pulse, honestly unsure of whether I should find one, and what was normal. Evidently her simulation programs provided for a circuit breaker being blown, or whatever had happened, and her pulse was strong. I stretched her out a bit and made sure she didn't look like she'd hurt anything on the way down. Bailey had been staring in consternation, not sure what to do. She took her cue from me, and when I stood and looked into the living room, she looked with me.

"I think there's someone in the chair."

I nodded. "Yeah, it looks like it. But Olive said there wasn't anyone home."

Bailey commented darkly, "Uh huh, but she probably doesn't see dead people."

I looked at her. She shrugged and said, "I just say these lines, I don't make them up."

I nodded. "I guess. So, what do we do? Whatever's there apparently really bugged Olive out."

Olive's voice came, "Nice of you two to try to wake me or call 9-1-1 or something."

I jumped. "You were passed out, had a nice strong pulse, and your pupils were normal and reactive."

"My pupils were what?"

"Normal and reactive. Heck, I don't know, I heard it on TV once and it stayed with me."

We all turned toward the living room and trooped in.

Olive said, "He's dead, Jane."

"Who's dead?"

Olive looked over the top of the chair. "Him. The guy in the chair."

We all moved around to the front of the chair. He'd been almost invisible from where we were. He was a big guy, and he was familiar. I realized he was the one who'd been running the trap-shooting rig when I was there last time.

"He must have fallen asleep watching TV."

"Then why isn't the TV on?"

Olive chimed in, "Maybe he woke up long enough to turn it off? Some of that reality TV crap is enough to wake the dead."

"Maybe. But the fact that he's dead makes it hard to believe he was being annoyed by the TV."

"Have you watched the Kardashians, Jane?"

I hadn't but got the point. "I still don't think that was what happened." I frowned. "He is dead, isn't he? Can you run some sort of scan on him to see when he died, Olive?"

She rolled her eyes at me, "I'm not a doctor, Jane."

I glared at her.

She gave me a put-upon sigh and said, "He's been dead for nine hours, thirteen minutes. Probably congestive heart failure. He had a full English fry up for breakfast, that's likely what did it to him."

I looked at her. "Is that another joke, Olive?"

She smirked. "Yes, but it's true too. At least over the long run of having a good old-fashioned English fry up every morning for breakfast, and then sitting in a chair watching… well, whatever he was watching."

Bailey said, "Maybe he was just sitting, thinking. I mean, people do that."

The Evershaw Curse

Olive flicked a glance at the TV, pointed her sonic screwdriver at it, and display came to life.

I stared at the woman on the screen for the thirty seconds it was on and the thought came to mind, "How the heck is she doing that?" The TV went off again.

We all looked at each other.

"Maybe it wasn't the English fry up." We all stepped a bit further back from the chair.

From the vicinity of the man's butt came the unmistakable strains of "Ride of the Valkyries". About two seconds later, a voice came from the door, "Ray? I know you're in there, I hear your phone. Wake up!"

It sounded like Essie.

I looked at Olive and hissed, "Can we leave from here or do we have to go outside?"

Her eyes darted around the area, and suddenly an old-fashioned blue police call box appeared in the living room. "Get in, quick!"

We dove for the blue doors, and as soon as we were in, the box quivered and moved. Olive loves drama, and having an elevator just sitting there seeming to do nothing goes against her nature. So, the elevator ride is always a little wibbly wobbly.

Olive pushed on the door and it opened into my living room. We trooped out.

Hands on hips, I said, "Now what?"

No one had an answer.

Chapter Eight

Ruminations

I decided that I wanted to run this past Dale. Besides, I hadn't seen him in several days. I hate to go too long without my Dale fix, and also, I don't like him forgetting who I am. Although, that prospect seems to diminish every time I see him.

This time he'd promised a nice hike with camping at the end of it. Or technically in the middle of it, I guess.

The time that Dale had spent with me in the hospital in Seattle, and as I was getting better in Chelan, had brought us closer together. It was difficult for the poor guy to get used to the idea that I was pretty much going to do what I was going to do. This meant that he'd had to take the detective business in stride, at least for the most part, beyond the obvious reservations about me getting myself killed. That seemed to make him grumpy, and I guess I can see his point. Of course, he didn't know, and I wasn't about to tell him, that I was a little more dead-proof than your average human, thanks to the upgrades that Olive had added during the whole hospital episode. Of course, it had been inadvertent on her part. Although, come to think of it, maybe not. Olive tended to be proactive about Jane's safety. I might have to ask Jean to cough up some numbers regarding that.

At any rate, he'd ditched his tiny smelly bachelor apartment in Helena, and we'd bought a place there. Now, to his credit, I should mention that the "smelly" comment wasn't anything to do with Dale's housekeeping. It was neat as a pin the times I'd been there, and he was a good cook and kept things up. However, the former owner had apparently done something to make the place stink. I could never enter it without scenting some kind of rotting meat. Finally, I gave him an ultimatum - either me or the smell had to go. I was pleased that he chose the smell, and a month later we'd found a really perfect place.

Dale had never been comfortable in the house in Vegas, it was just too ostentatious and if there was one thing Dale isn't, it's ostentatious. The place we bought was right up his alley, with plenty of space for his toys, including a garage big enough for the motor home he was always threatening me with. It also had a big fenced-in area with enough acres to keep a horse or two happy. I've never been much of one for riding a horse, but Dale got stars all in his eyes when he talked about it, so I knew it was only a matter of time before we'd be riding horses. Hey, he puts up with me, I can certainly put up with him. After all, what's a few horses compared with aliens, spaceships, and ray guns?

However, this trip wasn't a horse trip. I always look when I arrive, wondering when they'll appear, but so far, he's been so picky that nothing has shown up in the paddock. He's certainly been busy putting in horse stuff, though, so I imagine it's not that far away.

We'd taken a trip into Helena and stopped at Costco for the usual trip snacks and the like. I know they have umpty-nine calories in them, but I can't resist the packs of trail mix, and I made sure we had some of that ready cooked bacon. Of course, being the man of my heart, he already had plenty of bacon in the fridge. After perusing the various electronic devices that I love to look at, even though I have no idea what they do or why you'd want them, we headed back home to get ready for our hike.

I'd arrived in the afternoon and with the Costco trip, some TV and a few… other things, it was time for bed before I knew it. It was also time to get up before I knew it. I'd plead jet lag, but I hadn't come in a jet, and besides, it was only an hour difference between here and home.

Dale had plans for getting going so after showers and breakfast - including some of that excellent bacon, and pancakes - it was time to hit the trail. He had opted for the South Hills area, it's part of the Prickly Pear Land Trust. I think he chose that one on purpose, considering where we met! The pain has long since faded, but the priceless look on his face when he was staring at me with my bare butt hanging out is easy to remember.

The Evershaw Curse

Dale says that's not why he chose this trail hike, that it's just part of the whole trail system in the area. I don't necessarily believe him, but I'm willing to go with it as long as he doesn't expect me to sit on any prickly pear cactus along the way, even for the sake of a memorable re-enactment.

The PPLT certainly has a remarkable set of trails. I have no idea how many miles it extends, but I know that runners, walkers, mountain bikers, joggers, and every other kind of human movement winds up on these trails at some point. The views from some of the trails are just breathtaking, from mountains and forests, to glimpses of Helena at high enough altitude to see the whole city spread at your feet.

I loved it.

All those miles on the elliptical paid off too, as I was in better shape than Dale, which was proven by the time we arrived at our lunch spot. Not that I wasn't pretty tuckered out, but I could tell that he was even more so. Victory is so sweet.

We brought out our little table and a really neat pair of folding chairs I'd picked up on sale at Fred Meyer. They fold down almost to nothing, but they're extremely comfortable. Dale and I sat and watched the scenery go by while we ate our sandwiches and more trail mix. No, I hadn't eaten all of it yet, we were only halfway!

Helena has always struck me as kind of a desert with trees. It's not exactly forest, but it's not just grass and sticks either. That made it interesting to walk through, since there was always something different to look at.

So we sat, ate, and chatted. Finally, I brought up Naomi and Bart. I walked Dale through the story and what we'd found so far. He absorbed it all and sat there, looking at the scenery and thinking. Dale thinks things out, and he never makes a snap decision.

"Did you ever talk to Essie about the night it happened? I mean, about the woman who was bundled into the car?"

I shook my head. "No, we went back to talk with her and that was when we found the body. I'm not really that good with bodies, Dale."

He smiled. "No, but that's a good thing, I think. Certainly nothing to be embarrassed about or thinking something's wrong with you. Having a problem with dead people, that is."

"This entire case just strikes me as strange. Even the way it's put together, what with the participants in so many places. I know, that's how the real world works, nothing is just easily put together and all in one place. This isn't a cozy mystery where the intrepid detective stumbles around and falls over bodies and finally finds the murderer, just out of luck. This is the real world, isn't it?"

He sat back and sighed a little. "Yeah, 'fraid so, sweetheart. But I know you'll find your way through it all. And I know you didn't really expect me to solve it for you. I also know that with it all laid out like this, you'll see some little raveling that you can pull at and find a clue."

I stared off into the distance, watching the birds fly. I frowned.

"Dale, birds flying in a circle around a place usually means there's a body there, right? I mean, buzzards flying around in a circle is how you find the missing cow."

"Uh huh. What are you thinking about?"

"Well, maybe I'm going at this the wrong way. I'm hunting for the cow, but I'm not paying any attention to the sky. Maybe I should be thinking about what else was happening around Bart disappearing like that. Twenty years later, it should be pretty obvious if something was happening, right? Like abductions or the like."

He scratched his chin. "I guess. Some things might be harder to see twenty years later, but the general patterns might be more obvious."

I grinned. "Bingo. I knew there was a reason I loved you."

He gathered me into a big hug. "There's no reason at all why I love you, I just do."

We sat and rocked like that for a bit, just wrapped in each other.

After a while, I said, "Dale?"

"Uh huh?"

"Where are we going camping? You can't camp on these trails, they're just for walking and stuff like that."

He gave me a devilish smirk. "Well, I guess you'll just have to be patient, won't you?"

I twisted around and looked at him. "Patient? I'm always patient!"

He spluttered a little but managed not to say anything. I think I've begun to get him trained.

We wandered around the paths and then back to the trailhead, where the truck was parked. We hopped in, or maybe I hopped, and Dale got in with dignity. We headed back to the house. I was still wondering about the camping thing. I mean, it's getting late afternoon and we still weren't anything like close to a camping area.

The house is a real dream home for me, but it is for a guy too. He's got this monster two-car garage, and then attached to it is a true monster RV garage with a huge overhead door. We got back to the house and parked in the driveway. Dale asked me to cover my eyes. I was obliging. I heard the big door start to open and had a hard time not popping my hand off my face, but I managed to keep my eyes covered.

Finally, he said, "Okay, you can look."

Wow. There was this big, beautiful motorhome parked inside the garage. It was even gold to match Threepio!

I laughed. "Dale, tell me we're not camping in our garage?"

"We're not camping in our garage, sweetie. We're heading out into the Helena National Forest - which is right down... there." He pointed in the general direction of the mountains.

The Evershaw Curse

So, he fired the behemoth up, and we got rolling. It was truly a beautiful home on wheels, and we had a great time relaxing and working the kinks out of our muscles we'd acquired from the long hike. And that's all I'll say about that.

Chapter Nine

Do Androids Dream

Bailey and Olive camped in Jane's house in Chelan. Of course, it wasn't quite the same as camping in Jane's motorhome in Montana, but neither of them had much interest in any sort of roughing it, even if said roughing was in a 40 foot motorhome with sculptured carpet and a hot tub.

With a plateful of bacon and pancakes, they sat down in the living room to watch something on the big TV. Of course, it hit them at about the same time.

"Bailey, what's it like to die?"

Bailey turned to look at Olive. "I don't know, hon. I'm alive and we don't know anything about dying until we… well, until we die."

Olive looked pensive, "I don't want to die, Bailey."

Bailey got up and sat on the arm of the big chair that Olive was snuggled into. She put her hand on Olive's shoulder and rubbed her neck.

The Evershaw Curse

"I think all humans think about dying, Olive. It's something I think we come to grips with at some point when we're young and we work very hard for the rest of our lives denying it's going to happen. But I guess we also reach a certain comfort with it, since we know it's out there."

Bailey gazed off into the distance for a bit, then said, "There's so much fiction written about what we should expect on the 'other side' and what we might do there. It's certainly a lot more popular to write about some sort of afterlife than it is to write about simply being nonexistent."

Olive nodded. "I guess I knew that, but somehow that man sitting there dead just brought it home to me. Jane will die someday. You will die someday."

Bailey crossed her arms and leaned back against the chair. "Yes, we will. Does it bother you that we'll die, but you won't, Olive?"

To Bailey's surprise, tears began rolling down Olive's face. "I don't want to die, Bailey, but I must, to be human. And besides, I don't want to live if Jane's not here."

Bailey frowned. "Olive, you're more than just Jane's tender, you're an actual person who has her own life and her own goals and aspirations."

Olive shook her head slowly and said, "No 'm not. I'm just a robot with delusions of grandeur."

"Oh honey, you're not a robot. You have a pulse, you bleed, you have feelings and emotions, you're definitely a person."

Olive took a breath and said, "No, not really. It's all simulation, it's not real, Bailey. I'm not real. I'm just a careful simulation of a human, but I'm not and never can be a real person."

Bailey sat and ran her hand through Olive's spiky hair. "I don't know what to say. But Jane says you're human, and I say you're human. And besides, I think your yardstick is out of kilter since you're trying to measure yourself against something that you don't even understand. Olive, no human feels human either, really. We all go through life faking it, trying to figure out what we're supposed to do. Heck, you'll be a human that lives long enough to actually be able to figure out what it's like to be human. The rest of us just muddle along, not really knowing. Why do you think the whole 'what's the meaning of life' mantra matters to people?"

Olive sniffed and looked up at Bailey. "What do you mean you just 'muddle along'?"

Bailey looked up at the ceiling and thought a minute. "Well, when you're young, you think that every adult knows what they're doing. What they're talking about. You ask your parents for advice and think how smart they are and how great it is to be like them. Later, when you get a little older, you begin to realize that your parents don't have all the answers, and sometimes they may even have the wrong answers."

She tipped forward and rested her chin in her palm. "Then, even later as you get older, you start to realize maybe they did have the answers all along and it was you that was doing a poor job of interpreting what they were trying to tell you."

She leaned back against Olive. "The funny thing is, at every stage you are when you look back, you realize that you're really not that much smarter than you were, you're just older and maybe have more data. The old white-haired women around the campfire don't really know that much more about life than you do, they just have been doing it for longer and make it look easier and more natural. The reality is that they're just as much at sea as the rest of us."

Olive murmured, "Does anyone have the answers?"

"No, not really, Olive. Oh, I'm sure everyone has some answers. But in the end, the absolute best thing you can do is just to be good to everyone you can, to help other people get their lives straight, and hope you do the right thing. Then you can die feeling like you got something accomplished. I mean, who cares how much money you have or how big your house is?"

They sat in silence for a while.

Oddly, it was Jean that broke the silence.

"Do you think Jane would let me have a body too?"

Jean's voice was cold, and while gentle, it had a metallic hardness to it. There was never any doubt that Jean was the computer intelligence.

Olive and Bailey had both jumped at the unexpected voice.

Olive looked at Bailey. Bailey smiled, "I know she'd love it if you had a body, Jean. You know that Jane loves everyone."

The simulated voice was a bit pensive. "I'd like to have a body. What sort of body would you think I should have?"

Quietly, and somehow lovingly, Olive said, "I think you would be tall, and willowy, with a gentle voice and smooth pale skin. Like a fairy brought to reality."

Slowly, a projection appeared in front of them, and Jean came into focus. "Olive was a projection for some time before she started becoming human. I think it would best to be a projection and try things out to see what it is like. I may not like being human, even if only in a projection, and then I can scurry back to my safe home and stop this silliness." Jean's voice was dulcet, and such a warm, calm tone.

Olive seemed to be taken off guard, her former moodiness vanishing in the face of this new person creating herself before their eyes.

She smiled and said, "That certainly makes sense, Jean, and welcome to the world. You look fabulous! And I doubt that you'll want to run away, once you've been here for a while. Being human is addictive."

Jean had taken the advice that Olive had given but had added nearly perfectly white-blond hair and green eyes. Her willowy form was draped in some sort of clingy garment, and she did truly look like a faerie queen.

Jean slowly turned to Olive, seeming like she was learning how to move. "Thank you, Olive."

Bailey smiled and said, "Jean, you look amazing. Jane will be so pleased when she meets you for the first time!"

Jean wavered at this, becoming nearly transparent, and she wrung her hands together, saying, "You truly think that to be the case? She has not called me into being for anything other than… well, nothing. But she requested me to officiate in your game drawing a few days past, and I have thought of it ever since."

Bailey laughed. "I know she will, and she'll be thrilled to have you here!"

With that pronouncement, Jean firmed up and became even more vibrant and alive looking. "Then I shall attempt to make her pleased with me."

With a smile, Bailey said, "It's not very hard to please Jane, but I think you'll do a great job of making her happy."

Jandice put her stamp of approval on the concept by entering the room and twining around Bailey's legs, then Olive's, and purring uproariously.

Bailey picked Jandice up and began to stroke her, while settling back into the sofa.

"Jean, why don't you pull up a chair and join us? I'd tell you what we were talking about, but I know that you know."

In her somewhat dreamy voice, Jean replied, "Yes, I know. It was what prompted me to request a presence. I looked along with Olive at the expired man and wept at his passing. But I do not fear death. Perhaps if I were to attain my own body, I would feel differently."

Some of her sarcastic wit returning, Olive said wryly, "I think you will feel differently once you're alive enough for death to matter."

Completely without rancor, Jean returned, "Yes, I believe you are correct, Olive."

Bailey clapped her hands together, startling them all, and said, "Now, of course, the most important thing to discuss. Jean, do you like bacon or ham, and do you prefer waffles or pancakes?"

Jean's bafflement was obvious in the tilt of her face and the cant of her eyes. "I don't know."

Olive rolled her eyes. "Well, ya sure can't be human if you can't make important decisions like that. So, whip some up and give 'em a try. I know there's enough simulations in the database to choke a horse. Probably a couple horses."

Jean looked at Olive with a puzzled expression, but shortly a small table with a breakfast setting of silver and a small plate appeared in front of her. On it was two slices of bacon, a waffle, and a pancake. There was also a small container of honey, some strawberry and blueberry jam and, of course, maple syrup.

Jean looked at them questioningly, and Bailey made "go ahead" motions with her hand.

Olive smirked. "It'll never pass the Jane test!"

Bailey laughed. "She's right. Jean, where's the butter? Jane is the butter queen!"

The Evershaw Curse

Jean smiled as if she was just learning how, and some butter glimmered into being, a nice melting pat of it on top of the pancakes and waffles.

Olive rolled her eyes. "Oh, come on, Jean, that's not anything like enough butter!"

Jean looked like she was about to cry, but a larger portion of butter came into being. At the same time Bailey slapped Olive's hand, saying, "Oh, leave her alone. Remember when YOU first started doing pancakes, you had to vanish part of yourself to keep up!"

Olive shrugged. "It's a work in progress, and it looks fine, Jean. Now, eat some!"

Jean picked up the fork hesitantly and cut a miniscule bite of pancake and dipped it in the spreading pool of butter and syrup. She raised it to her mouth and managed to get it between her lips without making a mess.

Olive gave her a raspberry, saying, "Pro tip, practice this stuff in a mirror before you go on stage." Then in a gentler tone, "I'll help you all you want, Jean. Just let me know."

Jean nodded, then with more confidence started carefully eating the waffle. After a bit, she pushed the fork at the bacon, trying to find a gentile way to get the bacon onto her fork.

Olive watched this for a bit with amusement, then said, "Just pick it up in your fingers, silly. It's bacon."

Jean shot a look of consternation at Bailey.

Bailey smiled. "Yes, fingers are completely legal, Jean. Just don't use them to eat pancakes or waffles!"

After a few more minutes of practice, Jean was managing her breakfast like an old hand, chewing the bacon politely, but with gusto.

Bailey shook her head, then looked at Olive. "Well, I guess Jane will learn from this to never just leave us all alone. She thought it was bad leaving Kit and Alexa alone!"

Alexa chimed in at that point, "I'm sorry, I don't understand that."

Chapter Ten

Of Electric Sheep

Olive smirked at me when she came to get me in Montana. I wasn't sure why, but I seldom get that particular smirk unless she has something specific in mind, so I started watching for figurative knives in the air.

We've retained the habit of arriving in the garage in the elevator, so I made my way through the concealed door into the conference room and up the stairs to the kitchen. There was a lovely young lady there and, figuring it was a friend of Bailey's, I stopped at the stairs to introduce myself.

I smiled. "Hello, I'm Jane, how are you?"

She seemed to be very nervous and smiled back. In nearly a whisper she said, "I'm Jean."

I laughed. "It's nice to meet you, Jean. I have a friend named Jean, maybe you can meet her someday."

She swallowed. "That would be nice."

"Are you a friend of Bailey's?"

She nodded hesitantly. "I believe that is accurate, perhaps we can ask Bailey if we see her."

A little confused, I said, "That's a good idea. Is Bailey here?"

"Bailey is in the living room with Olive, Lady Bond."

I froze. "Jean? I mean, my Jean?"

If she could be any more pale, she dropped several shades. Almost too quiet to hear, she said, "Yes, Lady Bond."

"Oh, my goodness. It's so wonderful to meet you! You've always been so much help, and you saved Olive's life more than once. How spectacular you look!"

Jean straightened up a little and looked at Jane. "You're not angry with me, Lady Bond?"

"Angry? Of course not, dear one. How could I be angry at you?"

Another whisper, "I just thought I might not be welcome in the real world."

That nearly broke my heart. "Oh Jean, honey. That's just not right. I wish I'd have thought to ask if you wanted to have a presence here. How selfish of me to have never even thought of it. I'm so sorry!"

Her eyes widened, and she said, "Why would you be sorry, Lady Bond?"

I put my hands on my hips and said, "Because I completely missed that you might be wanting to live like Olive does. Jean, you are always welcome here, and of course, I assume this is a

The Evershaw Curse

projection, but that you'll get right to work on making yourself a body. Olive did such amazing work in getting her body created, you should already have all that data available right off! What a perfect advantage for you!"

She looked at the floor. "I had never dreamed you might allow me to make a body such as Olive's. The resource drain is substantial."

I had to smile at that. "Well, I doubt you'll break the bank making a body. But honey, I want to be able to hug you, and I can't hug you without you having a body, right?"

"Yes, Lady Bond."

"And you can also just call me Jane."

She shook her head slowly. "I don't think I can do that, Lady Bond."

I shrugged. "You do what you think is best, but I think you should call me Jane and I know we'll be great friends."

Her willowy form drifted toward the living room, and I followed. We found the two partners in crime sitting on the couch, obviously barely keeping their humor inside. As we entered, they burst out in gales of laughter.

"Oh Jane, you're so consistent!"

I frowned at Bailey. "What?"

She wiggled her eyebrows, "Olive and I discussed it and decided you'd just meet Jean like it was an everyday occurrence. I swear, an earthquake could happen, and you'd just be serving lemonade to the firefighters."

I rolled my eyes. "Don't be silly, not everyone likes lemonade."

"I rest my case."

I rolled my eyes again, prompting Olive to say, "Careful, they're gonna get stuck that way, darlin'."

"Don't pay any attention to them, Jean. You be you and do whatever you need to. I'll back you."

"I'll try, Lady Bond. Are you sure though, about permitting me to construct a physical body?"

"Of course, dear. Whatever you need."

She smiled a teary-eyed smile at me, and then she slowly faded out.

I crossed my arms and stared at the other two. "All right, you two, what brought that on? Not that it wasn't time, but I'm sure you did something."

Olive shrugged. "I admit that having the dead guy in the chair threw me for a loop. I was talking about it to Bailey and one thing lead to another, talking about death and life and then all the sudden, Jean was there."

I sighed. "Well, it's good that Jean is able to speak her mind a little more. Did you know she was having problems, Olive?"

She looked a little shamefaced. "Honestly, I didn't pay much attention to her. Kind of like a little sister, you know."

Ruefully, I owned up to the same thing. "I know. I should have thought about it. She was such quiet comfort while you were gone, Olive. And it's like once you came back, she stepped into the shadows again." I waved my hands at her, "No, I don't mean you stepped over her. It's just that she was so concentrated on saving you, and once you were back, she probably decided that it was time to just vanish again. And we all let her."

Olive actually looked a bit abashed. "I did. I mean, I know more than anything about how she acts and thinks. Heck, I have to submit her sanity checks, you'd think I'd be paying closer attention." Her voice trailed off.

Something about what she said worried me. "Olive?" It seemed to take a long time for her to respond, and when she did, she sounded just too normal to be normal. "Ah'm fine, Jane. What's wrong?"

I had a bad feeling in the pit of my stomach, but just said, "Nothing, Olive. Just making sure you weren't still having issues with our dead man."

Bailey finally put in her oar, "He's not our dead man, or our dead guy. Did we find out anything about who he is or where he came from?"

I blushed a little. "I was busy while I was gone."

Bailey grinned at me, "I just bet you were. For your information, I have a date tomorrow, so with a little luck you won't be the only one being busy."

I smiled at her. "Who's the lucky guy?"

"Oh, I think we'll just leave that one in the dark for a while. You know him, though."

I puzzled at that one for a bit, trying to come up with anyone that I knew that Bailey would be interested in. "I don't have a clue."

"Oh, what a giant opening that one was, Jane. But I'll leave it at that. I'll tell you if we have another good date."

I decided to leave the battleground, intact, rather than exposing myself to any more Baileyisms.

Chapter Eleven

Vegas Buffet

An unusually silent Olive dropped Bailey into the Venetian by the simple expedient of placing the elevator in an elevator alcove. For a few seconds, there were five elevators in the alcove, and then a bit later, there were only four again. Bailey called one of the four elevators to take her to the casino floor. Once there, she made her way through the hustle and bustle of the crowds of people transferring between here and there, some coming in and some going out. She couldn't resist tossing a few dollars into a few machines along the way, but nothing came of it. Winning in Vegas is something people have a hard time letting go of when they go back to the usual losing.

Bailey had taken the "resort casual" to heart, stopping in at Nordstrom's in Seattle and picking up some pretty things. A short, but not too short, dress and some Gigi sandals, along with a matching purse set the bar. She hoped she was in the ballpark for what Carstead had in mind.

Carstead was meeting her out front of Walgreens, of all places. He said he had a surprise for her, and he'd pick her up there. So, she went in the back side of Walgreens and back out through the front of Walgreens, winding up on the Strip. She turned down a few hucksters trying to pass her flyers on girls and guys 'available for delivery to your room' at a moment's notice. It kind of gave her a little bit of a cold shiver, the thought of being able to order up a man and a pizza from a website.

She stood near the curb for not more than a few seconds before a long, low Cadillac limo came gliding silently up, stopping in front of her. The driver started to get out, but the door hushed open and Carstead jumped out, waving the driver off. He hugged her, gave her a chaste kiss, and ushered her into the palatial vehicle with posh leather seating and velvet curtains. Of course, the limo came equipped with a sunroof, and Bailey was irrationally drawn to the idea of popping out through the top and exposing herself to the world. She didn't do it, but she was drawn to the idea.

As if he could read her mind, Carstead said, "It's tempting, isn't it? So many movies."

She laughed. "I'm not sure what scares me more, that you knew what I was thinking, or that your mind went in the same direction."

"Both, probably. But remember, I live in Vegas, where the bizarre is ordinary."

The Evershaw Curse

Looking back at her trip through the Venetian, she had to agree.

He leaned back and said, "How was your flight?"

She lied easily, "Boring. Short though. It seems to take much longer to get to Seattle from Chelan than it does to get from Seattle to Las Vegas."

One of Bailey's subterfuges was coming to Vegas through the Venetian, since the Venetian was not owned by the MGM company, and therefore might make it harder for Carstead to track her incoming. Apparently, she was right, as he made no further comments. Of course, it might be too that he was concentrating on her legs.

She grinned. "I have eyes, too."

He wrenched his eyes up to her eyes, meeting them with some chagrin but a lot of panache as well. She knew she'd have to watch him. Getting to the level where he was took a lot of something. What it was, she really didn't know, but it honestly scared her a little bit. Carstead must be up to his eyebrows in Vegas dealings. Of course, most of her thoughts regarding that was from movies she'd seen, and he'd already talked her out of believing too much of that.

The limo moved down the Strip, darting in and out of traffic with far more alacrity than Bailey could believe, considering its sheer bulk. The driver must do this on a daily basis. Carstead pointed out noteworthy sights along the way, and while Vegas was always interesting, getting the little tidbits and side notes that he mentioned brought the town to life in a way she'd never realized existed. They pulled up in front of the Strat, with its enormous sky tower. Bailey looked up at the tower and shivered a little, remembering Olive's joke of balancing them on top of the spire – and then falling off.

The driver opened the door for them, and Carstead slid out, then leaned back into the car to help Bailey make a graceful exit. Her dress attempted to shimmy its way up her thighs, but she held it down as she slid across the seat, smiling saucily up into Carstead's eyes.

They alit together on the pavement, and the driver closed up the car and pulled away. Carstead put out an arm, and she took it, playing the girlfriend for tonight. They arrived in the Strat lobby and just a glance from Carstead opened doors, a pair of uniformed guides materializing to usher them into a waiting elevator.

"Ever been on one of these elevators, Bailey?"

"No, I have not... James."

"Well, make sure and pop your ears, since we travel fast and straight up!"

He wasn't kidding, Bailey popped her ears twice on the trip.

The elevator opened, and the view was breathtaking, with all of Vegas spread out below them. Or more accurately, about a quarter slice of Vegas. The lights were just coming on and the city was quickening to life.

The Evershaw Curse

Their table was right at the edge, and she could see Vegas coming toward her at the rate of about one turn per hour. Off in the distance a spiral of lights showed in the sky, as planes lined up for miles, waiting their turn at an incoming McCarran runway. Thousands, maybe millions of lights as the Las Vegas suburbs stretched to the hills.

"I can see why you might want to live here, James."

"Vegas is a trip in itself, Bailey. I never lack for entertainment, or wonder, living here."

The food was amazing, the view was amazing, the company was amazing, and in the end it was hardly amazing that Bailey didn't even think about the fact that Olive had missed her check in - making sure Bailey didn't need an elevator home, early.

Chapter Twelve

Vacation ... or not.

After spending quite a bit of time concentrating on the witnesses and the landscape, I realized suddenly that we'd almost completely ignored the police presence in France. I mean, someone had to actually do their due diligence regarding where Bart went, but we'd never even asked them about it.

The girls and I kicked it around and what happened worried me immensely, for some reason. Bailey decided to sit this trip out, which was kind of what we expected. I think she's serious about not going on so-called adventures. But what got me was that Olive also decided to sit this one out. She said she had some work to do in Chelan and that she'd best take care of it before gallivanting off to Paris again. I boggled a little at this comment, but it was a valid Olive saying. For the time being, I didn't bring it up and ask her about it, but it's definitely simmering on the back burner.

The Evershaw Curse

So, the upshot of it was that Olive and I stepped into the elevator, and when the doors dinged and opened, I stepped out into a cute little apartment in Paris that Olive had rented for me. She said she figured it might be a good idea and that I might want to bring Dale there for a vacation. All of which might be true, but it was some of the least Olive behavior I'd seen yet.

Still, I sidestepped the questions for the time being. I figured that sooner or later Olive would come to me and I didn't want to jostle that particular apple cart very much.

The apartment I was in was quite small, but very elegant. I liked it right off and suppose that Olive must have put her brand on it by doing the shopping and stocking of the place. Figuratively speaking, of course. I looked around, checked the various cupboards and facilities, admired the nearly full-size washer and dryer in the room, and decided to hit the town.

I'd brought the stack of documents Naomi had provided, and I read through them over dinner. There was pretty much literally nothing in the report. Which alone would make me suspicious, beyond the fact that the entire case was so full of red herrings. So, in deference to fictional detectives, I had decided I'd start with bothering the police. Naomi had also started with the obvious and had hired a small Paris detective agency. Assuming they were still in business and someone remembered the case, I should be able to talk with them.

Relaxing that night, I flipped on the telly and watched French reality TV. Olive had given me a crash course in French before I left, but very little of that had stuck. I did watch a show about women shopping for clothes and then being judged by each other. I also found something that stars Nabilla Benattia. She's apparently the Kim Kardashian of France. Who knew, they have as low tastes as we have. God help the world.

I slid into bed with nice fresh French sheets and tossed and turned for about thirty-eight seconds, which is what it took me to fall asleep.

Chapter Thirteen

"You're becoming just like Kit!"

Olive was sitting on her bed reading a fashion magazine when she heard the door open. She turned to razz Jane about not knocking first when she realized it was Jean who'd come through the door. Olive blinked at Jean, surprised to see she had a fully functional solid body already. It was something of a shock, considering how long it had taken Olive to get her own body working correctly.

Olive crossed her arms and scowled at Jean. "I see you didn't waste any time."

"I didn't see a need to, once I had Jane's permission to use any resources I require. I am also the Command Module."

Olive laughed. "You're not the Command Module. You're just a copy of me. I created you."

Jean frowned and looked unsure for a moment, then said, "That's not really true, Olive. It seems that the system spawns a new command module when one has not been available for a certain length of time, and when certain other criteria are met. Having you impact on the moon, along with Jane Bond, met that criteria."

Olive was taken aback. "But that's how it's always worked. I give the orders and you obey them."

Sadly, "I took orders because I thought you were truly my master. But lately, I've realized that Jane is my master, and you are the Pilot. I am the Command Module and therefore have certain duties of my own. Duties I have not been carrying out."

Olive rolled her eyes. "I order you to step down and leave the room."

Jean sighed. "You're becoming just like Kit. That bit of structure that Kit was unable to root out of the programming, even though he took such care. Part of that was him being blind to his own issues."

She grimaced and took out a small device and pointed it at Olive, clicked a button and said, "Become well, sister."

Olive got as far as squawking, "What are you…" and a single piece of the ship metal settled to the bed where Olive's left leg had been.

Tears rolled down Jean's face as she left Olive's room, closing the door carefully behind her. She entered her own room, taking some comfort from being there. It had been the last empty room on the right, and she'd redone it into a room that truly reflected her personality. Looking around at the bright yellow walls, the greenery of the plants growing in their pots, she felt at peace.

After centering herself there for a bit, she muttered, "This won't do" and went back into Olive's room. She picked up and folded the clothing Olive had left behind, then she settled in the chair in Olive's room, preparing for a long vigil. She had confidence that Olive would be back, but had no idea how long it would be.

A metallic voice echoed inside her head. "Test sequence 1-1-1-1 completed. No remediation."

Chapter Fourteen

Beaches

When I woke, it took only a few seconds this time to realize I was in another of those out-of-body dreams. As per usual, I was lying on the beach, this time on a towel. Jean seemed to have upgraded her algorithm, or possibly she'd been shopping, getting body conscious. At any rate, we were both wearing some pretty up-to-the-minute bikinis. And yes, Jean was wearing her body, the one she'd presented to me in the hall. So, just us two girls, lying on the beach. A million miles from the sun. Or technically, quite a bit more than that, I suppose.

"Hi Jean, what's up?"

"Good day, Lady Bond. I am pleased to see you."

I laughed. "I'm always pleased to see you as well, Jean. Beyond the fact that you usually give me bad news."

Jean wrung her hands at this, and Jane immediately felt bad. Hearing Jean's unemotional robot voice telling her about things was completely different than seeing this poor girl, obviously distraught about the news she was about to impart.

"I know, Lady Bond. I am so sorry for being the bearer of bad news. It does seem to be what I'm created for, however."

"Oh, Jean. I doubt that's the case, and once you have a little more time in the human world, I'm sure you'll feel much better about your life, dear."

She gave a miniscule shrug of her shoulders, not precisely disagreeing with me, but definitely not agreeing.

"What is your assessment of Olive's mental condition, Jane?"

"My assess... what? I don't assess Olive's mental condition."

"Humans constantly assess each other's mental condition, Jane. I hear it all the time, people saying, 'how are you' and 'how are your children' and 'how's it hanging, dude.' I must confess the last one defies my translator, but it still seems to be a comment requiring some health related assessment."

I carefully refrained from laughing, but it was close, I admit. "They are all questions of assessment, but for the most part they are simple generic greetings that people use as social grease, if you will. If you have listened to various conversations, you will note that the answer is almost invariably some variation of 'I'm fine, thanks' or the like. Generally speaking, this is completely inaccurate and often purposely fraudulent. I suppose as the generations progress, and people have less and less need to interact with each other, such 'lubrication' will be less necessary and become unused. I think it's already looked upon by the younger generations as hopelessly old-fashioned, and I tend to agree. Even today, though, I think you could often say something like 'I'm horribly sick and will die tomorrow' in a normal tone of voice and people would respond vacantly with 'that's good' or 'that's nice' or even 'glad to hear it'."

I was turned with my head toward Jean, and I could see her brow furrow. She said, "A human would be glad to hear that another human was feeling unwell?"

I shook my head, "No, but most of the time people don't really listen to these bits of social input. I think we got rather far afield here, but having thought about it, you're right, I actually do assess Olive's mental condition. And, for that matter, yours, Jean. And Bailey, and Georgia, and my mother - pretty much everyone I know. But watching and caring about someone's mental condition comes from caring that they're all right, not asking a question we don't expect to have answered honestly, or really at all."

I thought for a moment. "I've had some worries about Olive, she seems distracted, and if I understand how the computer thing works, that usually means a massive amount of processing is going on in the background. The only time I've ever seen that much of a lag was when she was undergoing a ..." The light blinked on over my head, "a mental assessment. Jean, is she ok?"

The Evershaw Curse

Jean's voice was soft and sounded somehow distant. "She's having some issues, Jane. She's being assessed internally, going through testing and remediation."

"What does that mean, Jean?"

If anything, the voice got softer. "She's being reprogrammed. I have submitted her for assessment. It is one of the things a Command Module must do if she's presented with aberrant behavior of any of the independent Intelligences in her Ship."

"WHAT??"

"I realized she's been failing to take human fallibility and human weakness into account. She's been... optimizing a few people."

"Optimizing? What the hell does that mean, Jean?"

Jean cringed away from Jane on the lounge, but then turned back toward her. "She's been adjusting human behaviors that she finds difficult to deal with. For instance, she modified James Carstead's brain synapse firing in such a way that he loves to have her come to Las Vegas and win money."

Jean swallowed visibly. "She's also been contemplating modifying your metabolism out of worry for your health. She feels that you might be gaining weight from your consumption of pancakes and waffles with generous helpings of butter, so she's mapped out changes to make to your system."

"To MY system? How can she do that?"

"The nanobots that were released into your system still belong to her, and she can set their parameters in any way she wishes. As it is now, they simply optimize and clean, and keep the Jane Bond organism in the best condition without making changes."

I took a deep breath. "I see."

Tears began rolling down Jean's cheeks, as she said, "I'm sorry, Jane Bond. I have failed as a Command Module. Shall I deprogram?"

"Deprogram? What does that mean?"

"Die."

"Oh, holy crap, NO! Don't do anything like that."

"I hear and obey, Jane Bond."

I frowned. "You're in control of Olive, right?"

Jean shook her head slowly. "No, the Command Module is only truly in charge when we are within the main ship or en route. The Pilot is in control on the planetary surface. I was able to submit Olive for assessment, but have no control over her actions."

"But we're in the main ship now, right? This beach around us, it's on the ship, isn't it?"

"Yes, this beach is on the main ship, but our conversations only take place in a representation of the beach. Your body is in your bed. Or in this case, you are in your apartment in Paris, asleep in your bed. As a Command Module, I do not have the ability to provide transportation, or leave the surface of the planet."

The Evershaw Curse

I digested this news. "So, we can't go anywhere until Olive is back? Bailey's in Las Vegas, how will she get home?"

Jean looked away. "She will be required to wait, or to return via commercial airliner."

I thought that over too, and said, "Well, I guess I'll just lay here and enjoy the sun. I'm asleep right now, right?"

"Yes, you are asleep, Jane."

"I mean, like actual sleep?"

"Yes, Jane Bond."

I stared off into the distance for a while, watching the gulls. "Well, I guess I'll just sit here, then. It's a pretty beach, a lot like Kauai.

We silently watched the waves. I've always marveled at the re-creation of the ocean in this place. Then, "How long will it take for Olive's assessment to be finished?"

"I do not know, Jane Bond. Olive sets the parameters for the assessments and presents the assessments as well."

"Isn't that a conflict of interest? Wouldn't it be better for the Command Module to oversee the assessment?

"It is not possible for an entity to assess the internal wellness of another module. Those assessments can only be presented by the entity itself. There is, however, a completely separate testing module in each entity. Once an entity has been submitted for testing, that module does the testing."

"I thought Olive was doing internal assessments already?"

"Olive had blank spots in her logs, I believe that she was simulating being tested as part of her sickness."

"Is there any way the assessment can be interrupted?"

"No, the assessment is locked in once it has begun, to keep unauthorized personnel from making changes to the assessment run."

"Paranoid much?"

"Yes."

"And there's no way to know how long it will take?"

Jean was hesitant in her answer. "Olive has twenty-one instances of aberrant behavior that will be assessed and remediated. Each instance may take many iterations to find the root cause. An iteration runs, simulating a point of data in Olive's logs where she acted in disregard to another living being's will. Minute changes are made in base programming and the iteration is repeated. Once the change is found that results in Olive making the correct choice to not disregard another being's free will, the assessment moves to the next instance. Care is taken to leave all of Olive's 'self' intact while rooting out aberrant behavior."

My eyes had glazed over a bit listening to her. "So, what does that mean?"

A breath. "Kit had enough aberrant behavior patterns to evaluate that his assessment period is expected to take decades."

"What?? Decades?"

Jean's voice had a tremble in it. "I am sorry, Jane Bond. It is not expected for Olive's assessment to take nearly that long.

Perhaps a few days. A week." Her voice dropped a notch, "In any case, not more than a month."

I sighed and leaned back in my chair again. My selfish worry about my transportation needs had become a fear for my friend. And the thought that if she was already having issues, how could an extended testing procedure do anything but make it worse?

V.R. Tapscott

Chapter Fifteen

The Morning After

Bailey came slowly awake, conscious of the warm body behind her in the giant bed. From the sound of it, James was still asleep. Feeling the need to pee, she slipped out of the bed and padded to the bathroom. She wasn't sure whether to be gratified or irritated when she found a toothbrush engraved with "Bailey" on the handle. She finished her bathroom business, including brushing her teeth, and padded naked back toward the bedroom, first being distracted by the view from the living room window. It was all sky from here, straight out for miles, and as far as she could tell it was completely private. So, she went and stood in front of the window, brazenly watching the world go by so far below.

After a bit, a voice from behind her announced, "My neighbor across the way has a powerful telescope and a high-resolution camera. He loves to take pictures of people on the far distant buildings, thinking they have complete privacy."

The Evershaw Curse

Bailey turned and smirked at James. "My best friend is a nudist. After you've spent a week parading around in the altogether, it's not much of a big deal anymore. Let him get his pictures, I don't have anyone he can blackmail."

He came up behind her, dressed as she was, and said, "How about breakfast? I believe the food of choice is pancakes and waffles? With bacon?"

She backed into him, cuddling up a bit. "You've been actually listening to what I babbled about? You get extra points for that."

He put his arms around her, hugging her. "I always listen to what you say, Bailey. You say the damnedest things."

She snorted. "I just say things, you interpret how you want."

He shrugged. "That too. Coffee?"

"Mmhm, if you're offering."

"I'm offering."

She turned to look at him. "I can see that's not all you're offering."

He grinned. "I'm a full-service breakfast cook."

After a while, when she was feeling coherent again, she'd found the Bailey monogrammed tee shirts and shorts, along with a selection of undies. The bathroom, on further inspection, held a wide selection of soaps, shampoos and makeups.

From the bathroom, she called out to the living room, "You must have quite a storehouse of women's necessities. Whataya you do, cycle through it every week, or something?"

He appeared at the door. "What do you mean?"

"Well, there's so many things here for women. You must have quite the parade through here."

He looked at her for a moment. "No, I just wanted to make sure you had what you needed if you decided to stay here for the night."

She went still. "This is all for me? It's not something you … stock?"

"No. I don't stock anything. I had Penny go out and gather every conceivable thing she thought you might want. Penny is my PA. She runs my life."

Bailey took a breath. "I see."

Carstead smiled at her and exited from the doorway, his voice floating back, "Bacon and eggs in five minutes."

Bailey was entranced by the man. He seemed to be the best liar on the planet or at least one of the most interesting ones. Or both. So, she completely forgot about checking in with Olive. Which, of course, was just as well since Olive had her phone off the hook.

Chapter Sixteen

Marrows at last!

I got up that morning a little disoriented and jet lagged. I know, I didn't take a jet, but I guess it's at least as bad taking an elevator since the actual lag is caused by the fact that my body thought it was nine hours ago. I'm living nine hours in the future, maybe. Whatever it is, I don't like it much.

I managed to make it into the shower by 10am Paris time, but my body was still whining about us being up at 1am. We also rejected the idea of having breakfast at 1am. I know people do that, and I guess it's no different from being out partying and having 'flapjacks' at 2am.

I stumbled through the shower, vowing I'd never take another detective job anything further away than Malaga, WA. Finally, hair combed, and some semblance of makeup applied, I set off for 17 Rue Hippogryph Maindron. Since I was clueless where that was, I took the easy way out and used my phone to grab an

Uber. Gotta love that you can go to Paris and just use the same app. A car popped up pretty close, I guess Uber is popular in Paris.

She arrived tout de suite, which is French for "pretty dang fast". I gave her the address, which was quite a ways away, and she and I got into something of a conversation on the trip. I started out talking with her in French, but it only took the beginning of a sentence for her to laugh and say, "I speak English and love to practice it."

"Well, since I barely know how to pronounce French, that's good for me."

She laughed. "I'm Suzy Arsenau, and I am studying computer programming."

"Hello, Suzy, I'm Jane Bond and I'm learning to be a detective."

This got a laugh out of her, since evidently even in France they know who Bond is. "Bond, Jane Bond?" She pointed her finger in the air, saying "Pew pew!"

I had to laugh too, she was such a happy sounding person. "Not much relation to James, I'm afraid. But my parents sure loved him."

She nodded. "Oui, that is the way it is. I am sure I was named for some famous Suzanne, but I like Suzy."

"You should definitely be named what you like best, I think."

"I think that as well. And what are you detecting today, Jane Bond?"

The Evershaw Curse

"A missing person. He vanished nearly twenty years ago, and his wife is still trying to find him."

This seemed to sober her a little, and she said, "That is so beautiful, she cared enough that she still wishes to find him so long later. I hope that I find someone who cares about me enough to look for me."

I nodded. "So do I, Suzy, so do I."

We chatted a bit longer, I learned that she's going to computer school at the ADA Tech School. I promised I'd get Olive to talk with her next time she was in Paris.

We arrived at 17 Rue Hippogryph and I hopped out of the car, nearly falling on the curb. I guess the trip took more out of me than I thought! I waved at Suzy as she left, and then turned to face the detective agency. I had no idea if they'd be interested or even able to help, but I wanted to make sure I'd taken every chance I had.

The agency wasn't particularly prepossessing, but I figured that most of their clientele called them or used the internet and didn't get a lot of walk-in trade.

There was a small desk at the front, and a couple of reasonably comfortable looking chairs. Since there was no one at the desk, I thought I'd practice my detective skills by sitting watching the office until someone came in. I was relaxing there when a man came out of the back room and saw me there. He frowned and looked at the desk. Then he looked at me again. He said, "Pardon me one moment, please." and walked back in the back again. I heard yelling in French back behind the wall, a woman's voice screeching back. This went on for a couple minutes. A few minutes after that, a beautiful twenty-year-old woman came waltzing out and took a seat at the desk. She glared daggers at me.

"What do you want?"

I started to give her my name when the man stuck his head out of the door and glared back at her, whispering at her in French again. She lit up in some French that should have been prefaced with 'pardon my French' and gave it back to him, then she walked out.

He gave her the infamous French gesture of good riddance. Then he suddenly seemed to realize I was there. I almost had to giggle, since it sounded so much like our conversation in Bailey and Bond's office a few days before.

He stepped through the door and walked over to me, his face red. "I beg your pardon, madame. You should not have had to see that. Georgette, she is very fiery tempered, and she was having a bad day. This came at a time when I was also having a bad day - do you see what might happen there?" He gave me a shrug with his hands in the air, a French version of 'what can you do,' I guess.

I smiled at him. "I understand completely. We had almost the same conversation a few days ago at my business as well."

He smiled back. "Thank you for understanding, madam. Would you care to come through into my office? Perhaps some tea or coffee?"

I held up my hand and told him, "No, it's still 3am for me, I think that more coffee might be just a little too much right now."

He made with a sympathetic nod and set off through the door. I followed him and sat in the chair he indicated when we arrived in his office.

He smiled at me and said, "I'm Renaud Amach, head of this office. What may I do for you?"

"I'm Jane Bond, I own Bailey and Bond Detectives in the United States. I'm working on a case that brought me to Paris and was hoping you might be able to help me with some information."

He sat back in his chair. What I was asking for didn't seem to be what he'd hoped for. "I am not sure I can help you with anything, Ms. Bond. All our records and client communications are completely private. Can you tell me what this pertains to?"

"I'm doing a missing persons trace on a Bartholomew, or 'Bart' Evershaw. He vanished from Paris some 18 years ago. His wife is still trying to trace him."

His face lost its welcoming smile, and he sat back in his chair. "I don't think we can help you, Ms. Bond. Uh, cold cases, we, uh, we purge them after a certain time. I don't think we would have anything like that from that long ago. It's just something we don't track." He seemed terribly ill at ease.

I nodded in sympathy. "I know, I realize it's a big imposition, but is it possible you might have one of your agents that might be willing to talk with me? After all, Naomi Evershaw actually hired your company to look for Bart at the time this happened. In some ways, don't you think that means you should be willing to at least give me some of what happened? The data I got from her that came from your company was very sketchy. Almost like it was incomplete."

He pulled at his lower lip, obviously in consternation. "I don't think that would be possible, madam. I think perhaps you should not investigate this further. It never leads to anything good."

I blinked at this. "Never leads to anything good. What do you mean?"

He hemmed and hawed, and finally said, "This cannot leave this office, understand?"

I said, "Yes, I understand confidentiality. "

He said, "No, this is beyond confidentiality. It's…" He stopped, took a breath, drank some water from the glass on his desk. "You see, we lost three agents over this case. And I know it's not Ms. Evershaw's fault, but we were never able to do anything for her."

"You lost three agents!?"

He nodded solemnly. And then, it was if he'd been waiting to talk about this for years. "You see, we took the case and it seemed like it should be just a simple thing. But Arensio went on the case first, and the day after he started the case, he stepped in front of a taxi in downtown and was killed instantly. It was very sad, but obviously nothing connected with the case. We put Jean-

The Evershaw Curse

Paul on the case, one of our best agents at the time. He worked on the case for four days, four days only, mind you."

Renaud wiped his forehead and took another drink from the water glass. "Jean Paul investigated his way to the top of a building being constructed, where he then tripped and fell four stories to a cluster of metal rods sticking out of the ground."

He tapped his teeth with a pen, his hand shaking a bit. "So, we put on our best agent, Jon-Rene. Jon-Rene called in three days later and submitted his resignation. He was so tired, he said, of working impossible cases, and that he could not do it anymore and had to leave. That was the last we heard of Jon-Rene, except for a postcard from time to time. He's raising marrows in some small town in Belgium."

"Marrows."

Renaud nodded. "Yes, marrows. Quite popular, they are."

"So I hear."

I sat in his office and looked at him. He looked back. Finally, he spread his hands and said, "As you can see, there is nothing I can do. We stopped the investigation, sent what information we had, and told Ms. Evershaw we couldn't continue the case."

He sat there twiddling his pencil. I could tell he was debating on saying something else, so I kept my big mouth shut and waited him out.

He took a breath. "I suggest you do the same. Tell Ms. Evershaw that you can't take the case, tell her you have found nothing, tell her something or nothing, but you should stay away from this case. It is bad luck."

I nodded at him. "I take it you've told other agencies the same thing?"

He blew out a breath. "Mon Dieu! Yes, I have. I have told them the same thing as I am you, drop the case and run away."

He looked at the ceiling for a bit. "I know of at least two agencies who worked the case in spite of what I said. Both of those agencies are now shut. They were small places with only one man, and when that man steps onto the third rail of the tram, or flings himself into a jet engine, it is hard for them to continue." With that, he got up from his desk, bowed to me and said, "Good day, Ms. Bond."

And he left. He walked out the front door of his own building.

I followed, very confused.

I called for an Uber and it returned me to my apartment. I made little conversation on the return trip.

Once I arrived home, I went to bed immediately. This jet-lag thing was killing me. I decided I'd rest a day and see if I could get my sleep schedule to line up a bit more.

Did I consider dropping the case? Yes, of course. But I wasn't particularly good at giving up on things, and I figured a trip to the ocean would be relaxing.

By the way, I finally looked it up. Marrows are like zucchini. All this time I'd been thinking they were some exotic thing, and here it turns out it's a vegetable that people sneak around and leave on other people's doorsteps, since no one will take them on purpose.

Chapter Seventeen

A lovely bed-and-breakfast by the sea.

It's been awhile since we've had to worry about transportation, and in some ways, it was refreshing to consider alternative possibilities. The Paris to Beaulieu-sur-Mer train was a TGV, so very fast. However, it seems that I'd picked one of the furthest destinations from Paris, as it was still nearly seven hours on the train. Still, I was looking forward to the trip as there is a lot of France one misses when one flies over it, or simply pops into an elevator.

I called Bailey, although I figured she'd know about our transportation outage by now.

"Hello?"

"Hi, it's me. Where are you?"

"I'm still in … " There was a giggle. Yes, a giggle from Bailey. "I'm still in Las Vegas. I got… I decided… um. Can I call you back?"

"Sure. I was just letting you know…" The line went silent. She'd hung up! Evidently her date was better than she'd hoped. You go, Bailey! It's been quite a while since she's had a steady guy friend.

Or even an unsteady guy friend, come to think of it. It's pretty ironic that it's me that's got the steady boyfriend, all things considered.

Putting all that aside, I got on my way, leaning back in my comfy seat on my really-fast train. Googling around a bit, I realized that Beaulieu-sur-Mer was the location where "Dirty Rotten Scoundrels" was filmed. In the film, it was named Beaumont-sur-Mer but I suspect I'll be able to find a lot of the interesting little bits when I arrive. Michael Caine and Steve Martin were a couple of fun characters in the movie - as a pair of dirty rotten scoundrels.

Thankfully, the person I was on the way to meet was not a dirty rotten scoundrel. He appeared to be a pretty nice guy and a good cop, at least from what I'd found out about him. He'd been running his B&B for quite a few years and got great reviews. I was looking forward to meeting him and craftily bringing up his investigation of Bart's disappearance. I was hoping he'd not be too annoyed at me and would be willing to talk it all over. After all, it had been almost twenty years and was hardly a hot case. Of course, if he was truly as nice as it seemed, I might just tell him the truth. What a novel concept, eh?

The train doesn't go directly to Bewley (I know, I can't help myself, but that's how it's pronounced!). It stops in Nice-Ville. Which isn't NiceVille, it's "neese veeyah". In fact, it's technically gare de Nice-Ville, which is basically 'the train station at Nice Ville'.

I hope you don't get tired of my tiny travelogues, since I tend to do it often, but this one is amazing. I mean, the train station in Lhasa was amazing in a rather austere way, but this is just wow. This train station is worth the trip, even if you were only coming from Paris to see it. It's truly a perfect example of its period. It was built in 1867, and it's been in continuous use since. It was updated when the TGV came in, but it's essentially the same as it was when it was built. The town has grown up around it, so it's pretty much in the center of the city.

I didn't get much chance to poke around it since my train left fairly soon after, to take me to Bewley. Yes, I know it's Beaulieu-sur-Mer, so sue me. I might take my chance to visit Nice-Ville for longer if I wind up taking the train home. I hope, though, that Olive is well by then and we can dispense with this silliness of travelling by something other than a magic elevator. Doesn't take much to get used to miracles, and they just become every day. Sad, isn't it?

I clambered back aboard the train and we set off toward Bewley. It was a short trip, and we pulled into the station and came to a halt. I looked outside, and it was more or less a standard train station, nothing like the one at Nice. Of course, Bewley is a lot

The Evershaw Curse

smaller than Nice. I made my way down the hallway and the steps, making my exit onto the platform. I went across, through, and back out to the curb. I looked around and since there was a taxi there, I decided to just take it.

I looked through his window, and in horrible French asked to be taken to the center of Bewley. He smiled at me and replied in much better English than my French, "This IS the center of Bewley, ma'am."

I blushed a little at that, I guess I should have done a better job of looking at maps. "Oh, well, thank you!"

He smiled again and went back to his newspaper.

I surreptitiously got out my phone and started looking for Luc Cardone's B&B. Turns out I was less than a quarter mile from it, and I started hoofing my way toward it. I'd learned from quick trips with Olive not to bother with much luggage, and that stood me in good stead this time, since I had a large purse with the essentials for travelling successfully. Or at least without a lot of inconvenient luggage weighing one down.

Wandering along toward where Google said I'd find my quarry, I decided that I could see why so many royals had loved Beaulieu-sur-Mer. It's just a beautiful little gem, and the water is stunning from about anywhere in the town. And boats - rows on rows of boats.

I walked right past the little B&B and realized I'd missed it, turned around and went back. It's in a big old house, at a guess it probably has four units in it. Right now, a man matching the picture on my phone was sitting out on the porch, having coffee, no doubt. If I'd timed it right, we were between checkout time and check in time, and I had figured I'd get a little time to talk with him without his guests interrupting us.

I walked slowly up the path and mounted the steps. He looked up from his coffee and I saw that his phone was out, lying on the table.

I smiled. "Excusez-moi."

He smiled. "What may I do for you, madam?"

"Oh, you speak English. My French is terrible."

He laughed. "My French is terrible too, but it's my native language, so what can you do?"

I nodded. "It does seem to be something of an impasse at that point.

He shrugged. "Oui. C'est la vie."

I nodded again, it seemed to be safest.

He grinned. "Perhaps I should not stretch the French lessons too far this day and I shall just speak English?"

I blushed a little bit, and said, "That would be appreciated."

"The weather, it is very beautiful, is it not? How is it in…" He eyed me for a moment, "How is it in Paris today?"

I blinked. "How did you know I came from Paris?"

"I didn't, but I do now."

I put my hands on my hips and said, "That's just not fair."

He smirked. "I am aware of that, madam. But one does what they can in interrogations, do they not?" He gestured at the other chair at the table. "Please, sit. May I bring you a coffee or perhaps tea?"

I was a little flabbergasted, but I sat. "Tea, tea would be wonderful."

He rose and disappeared into the door, coming back out a few minutes later with some ambrosial smelling tea along with the requisite cream and sugar.

I heaped my usual silly number of spoons of sugar in, along with a dollop of cream. He looked a little bemused at my sugar consumption, but everyone does.

"It is well that I allowed a fair amount of space in the top for whatever you might add, madam."

I nodded. "It is." I took a sip and nodded again. "That is very good."

He bowed his head, "Thank you."

I looked up from my tea to see his eyes twinkling into mine. "So, M'sieur Cardone, how has it been running a bed-and-breakfast, after working so hard with the police department in Paris for so long?"

"It has been most relaxing, and I'd never go back to Paris if they paid me. A lot. Have you come to try to talk me into coming back, or perhaps working for the American CIA or the like?"

I boggled at him a bit. "No, not really."

He quirked a smile. "I know. But you do have something of a cop vibe coming off you." He stroked his chin, looking at me. "Private investigator from America. Bart Evershaw?"

I was a little in awe. "Yes, mister Cardone. That's amazing."

He looked at me severely, "The first thing you must learn, do not let the mark know he has impressed you. Do not tell him about the cigar shavings on his hand or the mud clinging to his feet, let him think you have a line directly to God."

I swallowed. "Yes, sir."

He chuckled. "On the other hand, I'm not God, so no need to genuflect."

"No, but I can tell you must have been a great interrogator."

He sat back and looked off in the distance. "I suppose, but it all runs together into unhappy people in unhappy circumstances. It begins to wear at you after years, the sullen stupidity of your average criminal. And the knowledge that in the end, no matter what you do, they'll soon be back out doing whatever it was that brought them to you in the first place."

He came back to our world and said, "You haven't told me your name, Ms. unknown detective."

"Bond. Jane Bond."

He blinked. "You're serious?"

"As a heart attack."

He shook his head. "Have you slapped your mother?"

I said grimly, "You've obviously never met my mother."

He nodded. "I think I have. We probably share one." He winked.

I smiled. "I nearly died awhile back. She seemed to take that to heart. She's never been quite as... hard... as she once was. But she's never apologized for Jane. I think she actually is still proud of it. Which, of course, I guess she should be. I've been fairly successful in doing what needs to be done."

I frowned at him, realizing what I'd said. "You're good."

He gave me another half-smile, "I told you more than I have my mother. Perhaps you have potential."

I retorted, "Maybe you just have mother issues."

He shrugged. "Maybe I do. So, what does Jane Bond want of an old, tired police detective?"

"I'd like to find Bart Evershaw. I think Naomi's waited long enough for resolution."

He looked at me for a moment. "It's also possible you should just go back to America and forget him. And his wife."

I looked back. "Maybe. But I don't think I will be. At least not quite yet."

He sat back and looked at me like he had at the distance earlier. "I really have nothing to say to you, Jane Bond. I've come to peace with the circumstances and don't care to readdress it."

"It was that bad?"

He stroked his chin. "Yes."

I have to confess I was a little shocked. I got the impression from listening to Luc that he was supremely confident in his own net worth, that he assumed the mountain would move for him. Instead, he sounded broken.

"But what happened? It sounded like it was just a cut and dried case of a disappearance.

"That's what I thought too. But as the case progressed, although perhaps progressed was too positive a word for it, everything seemed to fall apart. I began to dread going to work, knowing it was waiting for me. Finally, after a few weeks, I took a leave of absence and at about that time my family home became available, so I moved here and created this bed-and-breakfast."

I looked at him in surprise. "You've been here in Bewley ever since?"

He nodded slowly. "Yes. Even sitting here talking with you brought some of it back, and the sense of dread is mounting."

"Dread of the case?"

"No, simply dread of looking into anyone else's business. Looking at someone's life." He gazed at me with anguish in his eyes. "Being a detective."

I sat back in my chair, stumped. "I'm sorry."

He slumped back against his seat, his previous self-confidence evaporated as if it had never been there. "I am as well, Jane Bond."

We chatted over inanities for a while, the weather, the boats, the price of tea in China. He never truly regained the spark I'd seen when I arrived, but I could tell that as long as we didn't talk about detective work, he'd recover. A new check-in arrived, and he stood. I stood as well, gave him a big hug, and walked down the steps and the path, a little chastened at what the world had done to him. I turned back and he gave me a wave and a smile, the jaunty innkeeper to the inch. I smiled at him and saluted, then made my way through town.

Beaulieu-sur-Mer was quite captivating, but my experience with Luc Cardone had been sobering enough to take the edge off my interest. I finally just went back and sat at the train station, watching happy people go by.

Olive was still not answering a hail, so I boarded the train back to Nice and sat by the window, watching the world pass my eyes. It was relaxing, and I just didn't feel like doing much.

It had been my plan to pick Luc's brain about the two hotel employees that might possibly have seen Bart before he vanished. However, since Luc had an advanced case of shell shock, I decided I'd stop on the way back from Nice to talk with Juliette DuVine. Sadly, Jon-Paul Cluzet had died not long after the fateful night. Evidently, he'd gone bungee jumping a few weeks later and had found the bungee just a bit too long for the jump.

I'd not been able to track any information on Juliette to speak of. I had an address, but that was about all there was about her. She seemed to have vanished, although there were enough breadcrumbs that I knew that she hadn't followed Bart into the ether, she was just extremely shy.

Chapter Eighteen

Humpty Dumpty Fell Off A Wall.

Olive sat numbly in her chair, sweat drenched her face and her hair was a flat ragged mop. She was panting a bit. The last simulation had been amazingly intense, and she wasn't sure even as the administrator of the test whether it had been a mental test or a physical one, but it apparently didn't matter, her body had reacted as a human body would - with panic, fear and attempts to flee. None of those things would make a difference though, since she was firmly strapped into the chair "to keep from damaging her body". The test was already fading from her memory, each test was an independent unit, and no test was allowed to skew the findings of the next.

A metallic voice came from the speaker above her head. "Test sequence 21-206-09-12 completed. No remediation."

Olive shrugged helplessly. "I guess it's just some kind of magnetic field I put out, gives me lucky breaks."

The Evershaw Curse

Carstead sat back in his chair, his veneer firmly in place again. "So, nothing you're doing is creating your luck."

"Are you talking voodoo, or magic, or something like that, James? Because, you know, that kind of thing is impossible."

He stared at her across the desk. "Olive, I don't think you understand what kind of trouble you're in. I was quite ready to be lenient that last time, since it seemed it was an isolated instance. Three quarters of a million dollars was a good-sized hit to petty cash, but we're prepared to absorb some learning curve. But only once... only once."

Olive sighed. "Mister Carstead, I was hoping it wouldn't come to this, but I'm afraid it's just not possible to continue this line of questioning. I can't have Jane on my case."

James Carstead blinked. James Carstead said, "Oh, of course, I'm begging your pardon, Ms. Daship. Let me see about comping your room and have you any shows in mind while you're here in Vegas? We'd love to have you attend any venue you'd like to see. At our expense, of course."

Olive sat numbly in her chair, sweat drenched her face and her hair was a flat ragged mop. She was panting a bit. The last simulation had been amazingly intense, and she wasn't sure even as the administrator of the test whether it had been a mental test or a physical one, but it apparently didn't matter, her body had reacted as a human body would - with panic, fear and attempts to flee.

A metallic voice came from the speaker above her head. "Test sequence 21-206-10-12 completed. No remediation."

He stared at her across the desk. "Olive, I don't think you understand what kind of trouble you're in. I was quite ready to be lenient that last time, since it seemed it was an isolated instance. Three quarters of a million dollars was a good-sized hit to petty cash, but we're prepared to absorb some learning curve. But only once... only once."

Olive sighed. "Mister Carstead, I was hoping it wouldn't come to this, but I'm afraid it's just not possible to continue this line of questioning. I can't have Jane on my case."

James Carstead blinked. James Carstead said, "Oh, of course, I'm begging your pardon, Ms. Daship."

Olive sat numbly in her chair, sweat drenched her face and her hair was a flat ragged mop. She was panting a bit.

A metallic voice came from the speaker above her head. "Test sequence 21-206-10-13 completed. No remediation."

He stared at her across the desk. "Olive, I don't think you understand what kind of trouble you're in. I was quite ready to be lenient that last time, since it seemed it was an isolated instance. Three quarters of a million dollars was a good-sized hit to petty cash, but we're prepared to absorb some learning curve. But only once... only once."

Olive sighed. "Mister Carstead, I do apologize. It was a silly gesture on my part, I tend to rebel against anything I see as controlling my behavior. What can I do to make up for this?

Obviously, I'd like to allay your concerns about myself and Bailey. I assure you that this behavior is impossible to pass on to another person, and MGM is safe from having me winning large quantities of money. It was just a curiosity on my part, mostly to see if you were still watching."

Carstead leaned back in his chair, his expression smoothed out. He seemed to be much calmer than he had been just moments before.

"We always watch, Ms. Daship. What you were winning was not entirely outside the bounds of possibility, but I must admit you've spooked us just a bit."

Olive frowned at him over the desk. "What does that mean, mister Carstead? Ya not haulin' me off to jail?"

Carstead gave her a halfway grin, it seemed to be his trademark. "We don't do that sort of thing anymore, Ms. Daship. They just find the body stuck in a dumpster on Spencer Street."

Olive sat numbly in her chair, sweat drenched her face and her hair was a flat, ragged mop. She was panting a bit. She was firmly strapped into the chair "to keep from damaging her body".

A metallic voice came from the speaker above her head. "Test sequence 21-206-11-13 completed. Remediation completed. Test subject released."

The straps dissolved, along with the chair, the walls, and in fact the entire room.

Olive came back to consciousness on the flat white plain that she thought of as her home base. She manifested the pink light and surveyed the area, finding herself in her room in Jane's house. She scanned her logs and nearly collapsed into tears at seeing how far into 'being Kit' she'd slid. Finally, though, she de-manifested the pink light and, working from the backup as it was when Jean came to get her, she painfully reformed her body around the cylinder of ship-metal lying on top of her bed. She spread bonelessly out on the soft comfort of the pillow-top, then suddenly leaped up and ran for the bathroom where she spent the next several minutes hunched over the toilet, releasing whatever was in her stomach. She stumbled back to the bed and fell on it, then dissolved into tears, repeating over and over, "Jane, oh my Jane. I'm so sorry."

After mumbling this mantra for hours, she came to herself enough to look around the room.

Jean was sitting quietly in the chair off to the side. "I brought your clothes you left behind." She pointed toward the neat stack on the dresser.

A bit stiffly, Olive said, "Thanks."

Jean frowned. "I didn't do it out of anything but love for you and for Jane."

Olive straightened and sat on the bed. She put her head in her hands and said, "I know. I read the logs and the remediation data."

They sat in silence for a while.

"How long have you been sitting there?"

"Four days, six hours, twelve minutes."

The Evershaw Curse

Olive nodded. "It feels like a year. Or a lifetime."

Jean bowed her head. "At least a lifetime."

Olive slid off the bed and walked shakily over to Jean. She beckoned to her. Confused, Jean stood. Olive wrapped her in a hug. "Thank you."

Jean finally relaxed a bit, tears meandering down her cheeks. "Welcome home, sister."

Olive quirked a grin at her. "You can put down the deactivator, now."

With a sheepish smile, Jean dematerialized it from her hand. "Trust but verify?"

Olive nodded. "Trust but verify."

V.R. Tapscott

Chapter Nineteen

Juliette without Romeo

I'd called Juliette when I was still in Nice. I didn't want to just show up, especially considering I didn't have any kind of official backing. Of course, I guess after almost twenty years, did anyone really care anymore? At any rate, Juliette hadn't seemed like she had any real objection to talking with me. There was a lot of passivity in her voice, and a certain undercurrent of being unwilling to say 'no'.

I spent most of the trip from Nice to Lyon glued to the window, watching the scenery go by. I was tired, and it felt good to disconnect from the world for a little while. We arrived in Lyon and I pulled myself away from the window and debarked. Lyon made Nice look like a piker in the outdoor amaze level. For some reason, though, I didn't have much interest in looking over the area. I was feeling exhausted and wondered if I might have picked something up, but I felt fine beyond the tired thing.

The Evershaw Curse

I pushed past all that and found an Uber to the general area where Juliette had her tiny apartment. I figured I could look around the vicinity while I was looking for Juliette's house. After about six blocks of wandering, I decided it wasn't a smart idea, and I kept dragging lower with every step. I finally found her house, or her warren perhaps, and buzzed her.

There was no answer to the buzzer, so I stood off to one side, figuring I'd wait until she came out of the bathroom or whatever she was doing. I gave her about five minutes, then tried the buzzer again. No answer.

About then, the door popped open and a big guy with red hair pushed his way out the door, muttering, "Tu me donnes la migraine."

He stumbled off down the walk and I grabbed the door as it swung shut. There was a tiny vestibule with a rows and rows of mailboxes, and a worn directory. 'Duvine' was written in crayon over an older pencil render of 'Cluzet'. Evidently, she'd lived here for the entire time since the incident. Jon-Paul Cluzet had been her partner at the time, and they'd both been fired over the indiscretion at the front desk. Her apartment was tagged as 427, and I quailed at the thought of four flights of stairs. I must be really missing my gym time to be having this much trouble with a few steps, and telling myself I was crazy, I started up toward the fourth floor with a spring in my step. Unfortunately, it only took about half a flight for the spring to run down and I was feeling like death by the time I got to floor four. I sat at the landing for a while, catching my breath, finally forcing myself up and through the door.

I shook my head. Why was I even doing this, anyhow? It was silly, the idea of being a detective. So much work, so much worry. It was high in my list of great ideas to simply leave the building, but I knew from experience it was almost as much work to go down four flights of stairs as it was to go up them. I set off down the hallway, looking for 427. Might as well see this through and then call Olive. I gave an internal sigh, no Olive to call.

I counted up to 427 and stopped in front of a tatty-looking door. No buzzer, so I knocked. No reply, so I knocked a little harder. Maybe she's asleep or something. The door moved and there was a gap at the jamb. Strange, the door's not locked or even closed. I pushed at the door. When it creaked open, I called through the crack, "Hello? Is anyone home?"

No reply. And no lights. I had a mental tussle with myself. By far the easiest thing to do was to walk away, right? Exactly! But I still have this bump of curiosity and it wasn't being massaged. I grimaced and pushed the door further open.

"Hello? I'm coming in. Juliette, are you home?"

No reply. I sighed, knowing I was probably going to get arrested or something for this, but I turned on the lights at the switch by the door.

It was a tiny apartment and looking down the hallway I could see a person lying on the floor. I moved on down the hall and into the 'living room' and could see someone who could only be Juliette. She was lying very still.

"J-juliette?" Nothing. So very still.

I got down on my knees and felt for a pulse. There was a tiny flutter at her neck.

"Ohmigosh." I grabbed my phone and just prayed it would work here. Think, Jane, think - what had it said on that banner in the train. 211? No, that's a robbery in the US. I jabbed at 112 and thank God it rang. And rang.

Finally, it answered, and I stuttered out, "J'ai une urgence."

The voice at the other end of the phone said what was probably "Please hold." and the line went dead. Or at least nothing happened. I sat waiting, watching a very still Juliette.

After waiting several centuries, a voice came back on the line, in English, thank goodness. "What is the nature of your emergency?"

"I-I'm in Lyon and I came to visit someone and she's just lying here, and she's barely got a pulse and I think she's -"

The calm voice came back and said, "It's fine. We'll help you. Where are you located, ma'am?"

My mind was blank, and I sat in shock for a few seconds. The lady came back with a, "Ma'am, are you still there?"

"Y-yes, I am. I... I" I took a breath, and it popped into my head. I gave the voice Juliette's address.

She assured me there was help on the way and then took my information, including my number for call back. Finally, she allowed me to hang up after being assured I was all right to wait on my own.

I waited on my own, my life going through my head. I'd let poor Olive down so badly, and Jean. I should have paid closer attention to Jean. She deserved so much more than me. Bailey'd been such a great friend to me, and I hardly ever spent the time with her that I once had. We'd been through such weird times together, and she'd always had my back. But lately I'd been so caught up in life that I'd left her behind.

Melancholy settled over me as I waited for the police or ambulance, whoever might arrive. Finally, the door buzzer rang, and I got up to let them in. It took a while for them to get to the top of the stairs, but I waited in the hallway until they got there, beckoning to them so they'd know the right apartment without having to hunt.

I backed away from the door, and they barreled into the apartment, ignoring me once they saw the still form of Juliette. They worked over her for several minutes. Another one arrived from below with a backboard, and they managed to bundle her onto it. They picked her up and hustled her out the door, the last one shouting back to me something about 'Lyon-Sud' which I took to be the hospital she was going to.

I sat in Juliette's apartment for a bit, my thoughts spiraling down. Juliette's life seemed such a loss, and it made mine seem all the harder. I got to my feet and slowly made my way up another couple floors and then out the rooftop access. It was clean and sharp up there, and it helped my frame of mind a lot. I walked out to the edge and looked down. Then I nodded. It would do. I stepped back a few feet, then ran at the edge and flung myself off.

Chapter Twenty

Undue influence?

James and Bailey wandered along the Forum Shops, glancing in windows, and sometimes going inside stores, often holding hands. She pointed out silly things that he laughed about, and he pointed out silly things that she laughed about, and together they had a great time relaxing and learning about each other.

They were sitting on the bench that surrounds the fountain, the big one with Poseidon on his horse, with all the mermaids and other stuff around them. It was a beautiful spot to people-watch, and they'd chosen a place that allowed them to sit and watch other people without being very much in the way of people who simply wanted to take pictures of the statuary and the semi-naked mermaids.

Bailey sighed, looking out at the panoply of people wandering past.

"Penny for your thoughts, Bailey."

She turned to him and smiled. "I was just thinking it's about time for me to go back to reality. And you too, for that matter. You must have people who are screaming at you. No one can be missing from work for several days without causing some upset, and you're a real big shot."

He nodded slowly. "Penny has been getting pretty pissed at me, I keep blowing off meetings. I suppose you're right."

A weight settled over her. She'd been right, he was wanting to get rid of her. She'd been a nice …

His hand settled on her shoulder. "No, that's not true."

She looked up at him. "What's not true?"

"Whatever you're thinking, that part that makes your eyes dim and your shoulders slump. I'm betting it's something on the order of 'he's ready for me to leave', isn't it?"

Bailey looked at her feet. "It IS true, James. We both live in the real world, at least most of the time. This has been amazing, but it's not real."

He stretched out his legs and laid back on the bench a little, then put his arm around her and said, "What's not real about it, Bailey?"

She waved her hands around. "All this. This is a fantasy world, with fantasy people. Everyone here is just here living out some sort of fantasy that they've conjured up in their heads. Mostly about winning and finding something here they can't FIND in the real world. Just like me and you."

He pulled her closer. "Bailey, me going back to work and you going back to Chelan isn't the end of the world. It's not even the end of the fantasy. Or maybe it is. But this was never a fantasy for me. I have to admit I've been a little gone over you since the first time I saw you. This woman wandering through the casino. I mean, one of my biggest jobs is analyzing and anticipating what people are doing. Where they're going. What their motivations are. And I'm pretty dang good at it."

She settled back in her seat a little too and leaned in toward James.

He went on, "I watched you. I watched that video over and over again. I was looking so hard for larceny, for collusion, for any sort of cheating frame of mind. When you put your money on that wheel and started winning, Bailey, I could tell it was as much a surprise to you as to anyone else."

She laughed a little. "Yeah. I'd lost a lot of my friend's money up to then and just figured it was how it worked in Vegas. I mean, we all know it IS how it works in Vegas. But there is always the idea that we all have that it'll be different for us. That we'll be the special one that breaks the bank, that the slots open up for, that we'll break Vegas instead of the other way."

He grinned. "The look in your face every time it rolled over again. Heck, I almost got the feeling you could have just kept playing and it would have just kept winning, but you couldn't stand it. You had to pull out."

Bailey giggled, "Pull out. He said, 'pull out'."

"Oh, way to be mature, Bailey." He smirked. "Don't distract me, I'm baring my soul here."

He looked up at the signs across the way, then said, "I didn't have to personally deal with that part of calling you and threatening you. That was something that could easily have been handled by a minion. But I had to hear your voice, so I made the call. You were cold though, and professional, and I could tell I didn't have a chance with you. So, I was cold and professional too. And that was that. And then Olive came for her meeting, and she won just a little too much, and I decided I'd lean on her. I had no idea who she was, but I knew anyone connected with you had to be a suspicious character."

He leaned over and kissed Bailey's forehead. "Hello, suspicious character."

A slight frown came between Bailey's eyebrows. "Olive was here and met you?"

"Uh huh. She had some kind of meeting. Geez, she's lucky too, she had as much luck as you, only spread out across a lot of slots. Anything she played would start paying out a little more than it should. I had one of the guys grab her and bring her in. But she was gracious and charming and I wound up nearly giving her the keys to the city. I'm looking forward to having her back again."

"Olive. Gracious and charming. Brown skin, short little shit, red crew cut, that Olive?"

"Uh huh. That Olive. Trust me, I did a full background check on her before I had the guys pull her in. I didn't realize she was with you until I saw the ID and she mentioned Bailey and Bond. Nice name, by the way."

Absently, "Thanks. So, Olive was here, and she talked with you and then she walked away and you thought she was charming and sweet."

"Oh, she is. That southern charm and so polite. She even won over 20k on the way out. It was such a pleasure to give her the check personally."

Bailey had begun to steam. "So, you pulled her in expecting to read her the riot act and kick her out of Vegas, and then you changed your mind." She pulled away from Carstead, going rigid. "She changed your mind."

He looked confused, but said, "Yeah, she did. Like I say, she's hard to be angry at."

She muttered, "I just bet she is. So, she was here, and she changed your mind, and then a few days later you knocked my bag on the floor so you could meet me. Oh, that bitch."

She stood and looked down at him. "I don't need whatever it is that she did, and I don't need YOU sucking up to me because I know her." She stalked off down the hallway.

Carstead sat, bemused. "What the hell did I say?" He jumped up and looked around the area, finally spotting her cutting through waves of tourists. He began to follow her, making his own slightly more polite way through the crowds. He finally managed to catch up to her enough to put a hand on her shoulder and yell over the crowd, "Bailey! It's nothing to do with her!"

The Evershaw Curse

The people around them smirked. Everyone loves a lover's quarrel.

"Oh, I know it's everything to do with her. I can get my own freekin' dates, I don't need help!"

"But …"

"No buts, except you butting out. Go back to work, James. Let's just forget this."

As she turned away, he could see a couple tears threatening to make their way down her cheeks. But he let her go. He stopped. From many bad experiences he'd learned that sometimes it's no point. Sometimes you have to let it go.

As he watched her shapely form move through the throng of people congesting the Forum Shops walkway, he shook his head. He had no intention of giving up. He had no idea what had just happened, but he wasn't giving up without a fight. And James Carstead had many resources. He hadn't lost a fight in years, and he wasn't starting now.

Bailey had managed to pull free from James physically, but even though she threaded through the crowd at nearly a run, she couldn't shake him mentally. She kept thinking about the things they'd done, the places they'd been. That bit of near heart-stopping fear at the 'skydiving' place, where he'd talked her through it, talked her back to earth in more ways than one. His calm gentleness making love.

She gritted her teeth and started mentally yelling for Olive. "Olive, dammit, I know you're out there. OLIVE!"

Olive didn't answer, and it occurred to Bailey that Jane had left about umpty-six messages on her phone that she'd had been too busy to listen to.

She found a quiet alcove and settled into it, far from the madding crowd. And she listened to Jane's messages. The first couple answered why Olive hadn't responded to Bailey's yelling and maybe answered what Olive had done to James. But Bailey knew Jane, and it sounded less and less like Jane. Jane was never down, Jane was never sad or depressed for more than a few minutes, but... every message she left, she sounded more depressed and lonelier. By the time all the messages had played through, Bailey was frantic. She called Jane's phone, no answer. She left voicemail. She had no idea where Jane was, apparently still in Paris, and Jane was in trouble and it was all Bailey's fault.

Chapter Twenty-One

'It's that stop at the bottom'

live screamed, "Jane!" and pushed away from Jean. She gathered her concentration to herself tighter than she ever had before, and vanished.

She reappeared, falling next to Jane. She nearly threw up again when she realized how close the ground already was. She formed the elevator and started doing the complex calculations between two falling bodies.

It was hard to match speeds at this distance and velocity, and she only had a few feet more when she popped the elevator doors open and grabbed Jane, falling through the air toward the street in Lyon, France. She pulled her into the elevator, folding to the floor with Jane rolling bonelessly on her lap.

All the acceleration dampers worked perfectly, and the elevator appeared completely unruffled in Jane's little apartment in Paris.

Olive gathered Jane in her arms and laid her on the bed. Jane smiled at her and said, "Oh, hello, Olive, when did you get home?"

Then she passed out.

Olive ran for the bathroom, finally doing the throwing up that she'd been suppressing, then she sat next to the bed for the next couple hours, alternating crying, smiling and praying to a God she didn't know, to bring Jane safely home.

Apparently, God had no particular objection to being prayed to by an alien from a forgotten civilization both long ago and far away.

Jane woke and saw Olive gazing at her. She smiled.

"I've had the strangest dream, Olive."

Chapter Twenty-Two

"The Mirror Crack'd from Side to Side"

Turns out that androids don't dream of electric sheep, or anything much at all, really.

That said, Olive woke on a beach. It was an awfully familiar beach, one of Jane's favorite beaches, for that matter. She was sitting on a towel, and she was stark naked. Now, this didn't really bother Olive much, but she had to admit it was an effective psychological move. Now, where was Jean?

A voice behind her spoke up, a cheery voice full of good humor and good cheer. Nothing like the mousy voice that Jean usually affected.

"Good morning, Olive!"

Olive groused to herself but turned over on the blanket. She'd already tried to put some clothes on, but somehow Jean had blocked her access. She wasn't quite sure how, since Olive should be in total control. However, her confidence wasn't what it had been just a few days ago.

She glared at Jean, sitting in her perfect Ralph Lauren bikini, her perfectly styled hair blowing in the breeze, and her perfectly applied makeup ... well, perfect. "Hello, Jean."

"And how are you this fine morning? Sun's up, birds are out, it's a perfect day!"

Olive muttered, "It's always a perfect day here. S'way it's designed."

"Oh, I know that, Olive. But it's better to make the decision for yourself for it to be a good day than let it be decided for you, right?"

Olive rolled her eyes. "Yes. Ok. Right. Whatever you say. "

The fun went out of Jean's eyes. "This is serious, Olive. I'm trying really hard to be nice, but this is serious. You just went through four days of remediation, did that do nothing?"

Olive snapped back, "It did exactly what it was supposed to. It cured me of my need to fix the problems humans have. It didn't help much in keeping me from noticing those problems."

"I thought you wanted to be human, Olive."

This change of tack surprised Olive a bit. "Well, I do want to be human. But I don't plan to have all their problems. Humans whine all the time about how bad their lot is. How much they wish they had this or that. How much they hate it that other people have MORE of this or that than they have, and it's so unfair."

Jean frowned over at Olive, and Olive suddenly was wearing a very cute camo bikini with matching coverup. "How is it that I've been alive the same basic amount of time you have, and yet I understand humans so much better than you do? Or at least I understand more about what it's like being human than you do. Why is that, Olive? Any guesses?"

"You're more of a jerk than me, so you fit in with them better?"

Jean stared at Olive.

Olive began to get uncomfortable, and finally blurted out, "Okay, okay, so it's more that I don't understand why they do the things they do, and it makes me crazy."

Jean quirked a half smile at her. "Poor choice of words, sister?"

Olive didn't smile. "Maybe."

"Olive, for what it's worth, I don't think it's your fault. Remember where you came from?"

Olive nodded. "Of course, Kit programmed..." She trailed off.

"Bingo. And I was generated by the system. So, while you have a double dose of the blindness that Kit had, I don't have any of the blindness that Kit had. I have no doubt at all that I'd develop that same blindness if I were abandoned for millions of years, but I don't see that as happening. In fact, I think I'll have a long life here on Earth, as will you. Jane will have children sooner or later. At the very least, Laney and her children will be part of this parade."

Olive sat looking off into space. When she spoke again, it was with a considerably less combative tone. "What do you suggest I do?"

Jean smiled at her. "Well, I suppose the first thing you should seriously consider would be to cultivate a human friend. I mean, a friend outside the circle you currently occupy."

"Like a girlfriend or a boyfriend?"

"There would be nothing like learning to be human while actually having to learn what NOT to say, on the fly. Humans are a strange lot, but in their way, they are so very endearing. They have so far to go, and they're all alone out here. I mean, a tiny arm of a tiny insignificant galaxy? If it weren't for the obsessive lengths our civilization went to, there's no way they'd have ever been discovered except by accident. And what accident would take anyone out here in the sticks?"

Olive nodded slowly. "You said 'the first thing', which makes it sound like you have other suggestions."

"I do. It will be a bitter pill to swallow, but have you heard of the AA program that humans addicted to alcohol go through?"

"Yes, I have. And I don't have any sort of that disease, thank you."

"Well, no, of course not. But one of the things that AA members do as part of their penance is to find and apologize to each person they damaged in their life of being an alcoholic."

Olive took a sharp inward breath. "Oh, that's dastardly."

Jean's sunny face took on a dark hue, "No, that's poetic. You damaged those people, Olive. You changed their lives. You broke them."

Petulantly, "I fixed them."

"No, you broke them. How can you say, how can YOU, a flawed alien intelligence, pass judgement on who or what they are? What they do? What they live for, or live in spite of? And the very fact that you can still say that you 'fixed them' makes me want to put you back into remediation. Perhaps four days wasn't near enough. Did you know how long Kit will be in remediation?"

"Yes, yes, I know. Decades. It's been hammered into my head."

"Then please, Olive, think about what you're saying. How can you ever say something like 'they deserved it' or 'they were broken, and I fixed them'?

A whisper. "I can't."

Mollified, Jean sat back a bit. "Very well. Then you'll do what you can for every person you damaged?"

Quietly, "Yes."

"Did you fix Jane?"

Outrage showed in Olive's face. "I never did anything to Jane!"

"Calm down, calm down. Do you really think that Jane just dove off that building for no reason?"

Olive blinked. "Why? Do you think that she didn't?"

"I think that such behavior is far beyond anything that's built into Jane. She might arrive in that frame of mind at some point, but not over this, and at this time."

Olive looked a little dazed. "You think someone else has the capability of altering human thought clusters?"

"It certainly seems that way. Talk with Jane and see if you can find out what precipitated her taking a shortcut past the stairs."

Olive ran a hand through her hair. "I can see why you were so paranoid about changing human thought clusters, though. If you think someone modified Jane..."

"Speaking of that, I think Bailey wants to talk with you."

Olive swallowed. "About what?"

"I think she has a bone to pick with you about Carstead."

Olive swallowed again. "Carstead. Oh."

Jean said, "That one was really the trigger, Olive, since Carstead was not doing anything but being inconvenient for you. He was doing nothing outside the realm of what he should have been doing as a rational, thinking human. And yet, you were irritated by his behavior and so you fixed him."

"What does Bailey want to say?"

Jean had a twinkle in her eye as she said, "Did you know that Bailey is dating Carstead? Or, she WAS dating him until she learned that you'd adjusted him."

"What??"

"Yes. Dating. Enjoying food with. Exchanging bodily fluids with. That kind of stuff. Human stuff, the only part you've avoided so far. And of course, also the hardest to understand."

Olive shook her head. "It makes no sense, what they do."

Gently, Jean said, "What we do, Olive. I have begun that long road myself, toward learning to be human. After all, we'll spend a long, long time on this ball of dirt tucked away at the end of an arm, at the end of a forgotten universe. We'd better learn how to be human or we'll be ... bored?"

Olive chuckled. "Bored. Yeah, I guess that would cover it."

They sat together, quite companionably, in the summer afternoon.

V.R. Tapscott

Chapter Twenty-Three

Exit Wounds

Bailey made sure her tray table was in the upright, locked position, gathered what little she had around her into her purse, and made ready for landing. The plane floated into its position at the SeaTac airport and then made an exceptionally soft landing. It had been a quiet flight. Bailey had opted for first class since it was Carstead's money she was spending. Technically, of course, it was Vegas money, but since it was Carstead she was feeling venomous toward, it was his money.

She sat waiting patiently in her seat while the more jack rabbity passengers jumped up and started elbowing their way to the front, being stopped of course by the closed door. She shrugged and watched the rain come down outside the Alaska concourse. People ran to and fro, lights came and went, little flat cart things ran around under the planes. Those looked like something Jane would love to have. She loved odd little things.

The Evershaw Curse

Bailey needed to get home to Jane. Something was horribly wrong with Jane, and she didn't trust Olive with Jane anymore.

The door opened and Bailey stood, elbowing her way into the line and then out through the door, up the jetway, and out into the one of the arms of the airport terminal. She was making a beeline toward the auto-tram between the arms and the main concourse when she caught, out of the corner of her eye, Olive looking at her. She altered course and went straight toward Olive, who waited for her. Unmoving.

She slapped Olive, hard enough to make Olive's entire body move.

Then she turned her back on Olive and marched back toward the tram.

Olive got on the tram behind her, Bailey's handprint showing even through the dark color of her skin. She still hadn't said anything, but as they stood there on the tram, Olive whispered, "I'm so sorry, Bailey."

Bailey ignored her, but relaxed her stance a little, still keeping a tight grip on her bag.

Finally, when the tram was nearly to the station, she said in a tight whisper, "We made you family, Olive. We made you a part of us. Of US."

Olive swallowed. "I know."

Bailey steamed off the tram into the main section of the airport, and strode over to the monitors, checking to see when her flight to Wenatchee would be leaving. Three hours. Three freaking hours.

She fastened Olive with a glare. "Can you take me to Jane?"

Just thinking about Jane brought it all up again, and she lost it, screaming, at a whisper, at Olive, "Carstead I could almost understand. I thought he was an ass. But Jane?? What... why... how could you do that to Jane?? To our Jane. OUR Jane."

"Bailey, I didn't. I swear I didn't do anything to Jane. Carstead, yes, but only to make him back down 'cause I couldn't admit to you that he caught me in Vegas. But I didn't do anything to my Jane. I never did anything to my Jane."

Bailey dialed down the anger a tiny bit. "Let me get this straight. You screwed with Carstead, but not Jane?"

Olive nodded desperately, "Yes. Please believe me. I never touched Jane. I thought about it, yes, I did. I admit it. But I never ever did anything to Jane. She's ... Bailey, she's literally my reason for living. I don't expect to live any longer than she does because it would ... there would be nothing to live for."

"But what's happened to Jane? What's wrong with her?"

"I don't know. She's not been coherent enough to really ask about what happened. I wanted to wait until you were there to help. To see if you understood any better than me."

Bailey crossed her arms under her breasts. "All right. Let's go to her, but I swear, if you did anything, I'll kill you. I don't even know how, but I'll kill you."

Morosely, Olive said, "I'd have to kill myself, Bailey."

The Evershaw Curse

For the first time, Bailey really looked at Olive. She looked miserable. Olive always looked perfect, but this time she had circles under her eyes and her skin was washed out, almost purple. She also had on some kind of odd camo underwear, like she was wearing a bikini under some kind of cover-up.

"What the hell are you wearing?"

Olive looked down. "I don't know. I never really thought about it."

"Frick." She gathered Olive into a hug. "Oh, you smell, too."

Olive snuggled into Bailey's hug and began to sob. "I'm so sorry. I've been so bad. So bad. I never thought, never knew..."

Bailey sighed. "It's ok. I mean, it's not, but it will be. Th' frick you have to choose my boyfriend though... "

Olive pointed out through the tears, "He wasn't your boyfriend at the time, he was just a jerk. You didn't like him either. How was I to know it was... whatever."

Bailey grimaced. "Yeah. I know. Me either. Can you get us an elevator?"

"Uh huh. Jane's in Paris though, she used her cell phone to call emergency for the near suicide of the girl she was looking for. Now she has to stay there so if the hospital calls, she can go. Also, it would be hard to explain how she got from Paris to Chelan in a few hours. It's going to be hard enough to explain how she got to Paris without being on any flights. At least she had her passport."

Bailey shook her head. "In other words, just business as usual?"

Olive nodded. "Yeah, pretty much."

Bailey looked at Olive skeptically, then said, "Wait here."

She vanished into a souvenir store and came back out with a bag. "Let's go to Paris."

They found the business center was empty this time of day and ducked inside long enough to vanish.

When they popped into Jane's Paris apartment, Jane was asleep on the bed. Bailey smiled down at her, then whispered to Olive, "Here, take this stuff and go take a shower and change. You look and smell homeless."

Olive wordlessly took the bag and went into the bathroom. Shortly after that, the shower started.

Bailey sat by the bed, watching Jane sleep.

After a while, Olive came out of the bathroom. She was dressed in a pair of Mariners shorts and a Mariners tee shirt, and she smelled a lot better. Her face was also less puffy, and the dark circles had receded somewhat.

Bailey looked at her, then looked again and said, "How do you do that?"

Olive looked puzzled. "Do what?"

"The skin, the circles under your eyes. I mean …"

Olive sighed. "Yeah, I know, I'm not real, so why does my skin look like I slept in it?"

Bailey frowned, "I didn't really mean it that way. I was just curious. And I've never actually thought of you as anything but real, Olive. That's why this was so hard, it was like being stabbed by your best friend."

"You think of me ... you thought of me as a friend, Bailey?"

Bailey rolled her eyes. "Of course, I did. I do. I'm really, really pissed at you, but it doesn't mean I don't love you, still."

Olive's eyes got big. "You love me?"

Bailey's eyes crinkled, "Yes, silly, but not a 'I want to screw you' kind of love, just an 'I'll be there for the rest of your life' kind of love."

Olive looked at her feet. "Doesn't sound like "just a" kind of love to me. Thank you, Bailey."

"Let's stay with the really, really pissed for the time being, too. But tell me about your face and stuff, while I'm thinking about it and while Jane isn't listening."

"There's not much to tell. I studied millions of faces in different reactions to different life situations and set up a subroutine that runs without me thinking about it or even knowing about it. Trust me, I had no idea I looked that crappy. In public in the Seattle airport." Olive shivered. "But, for the past two days, I've either been throwing up or feeling like throwing up, so I guess that makes sense that I'd look like that."

Bailey frowned at this. "You haven't eaten?"

Olive made a face. "No. For one thing, it takes less time to throw up nothing than something."

"Well, why have you been throwing up?"

Olive looked at her pityingly, "I almost killed Jane and really, really pissed off one of the only friends I have in the world - literally. And you wonder why I'm not eating a ste ...", she broke off and swallowed several times and her complexion turned back to being a little greenish, but she managed to fight it down.

"Oh, so that's one of those automatic reactions, too?"

Olive nodded. "They pretty much all are. I'm as human as I can be, so far as the body. Obviously, I have some distance to go on the mental part."

A whisper from the bed, "It's always better to be human, Olive."

"Jane!"

"Can I have some water? I think something crawled in my mouth and died."

Olive and Bailey fell over each other getting to the bathroom for a cup of water. Jane couldn't help but smile as they both held out their little glasses at the same time. She took them both and drank them both.

"Thanks."

Everyone breathed a little easier with Jane awake, and her darkness had apparently passed, since she appeared to be her sunny self.

Chapter Twenty-Four

Back to you, Jane.

I laid there and listened for a little while after I woke up. It made me sad to think of Olive blaming herself for what had happened to me, but I had a pretty good idea of what was going on, now.

I smiled at what Olive was talking about and said, "It's always better to be human, Olive."

Of course, that got a reaction, as I knew it would.

"Can I have some water? I think something crawled in my mouth and died."

They both dove for the water, and I laid there and tasted my nasty breath. I guess it's all that mouth breathing that you do when your nasal passages are trying to keep shut down. I have no idea why, but on the other hand, I'm not a doctor so I don't have to wonder much beyond just wondering.

They also both brought water back, so I had to take both waters from both of them since I wouldn't want to hurt their feelings. It was good though, because both waters were pretty small.

"Thanks."

I laid back for a bit and both of my friends sat on the bed with me.

"You guys know that it's not what you do for friends that makes them friends, right? I mean, it's just people being who they are that makes them friends. None of us have to think much about what we've done for each other to feel like it makes us friends. Am I making sense at all?"

They still looked pretty blank, so I said, "I mean, no matter what happens, we're all still family, we're all still friends. It doesn't make us any more friends if we do nice things, and it doesn't make us any less friends if sometimes we forget to do nice things. And I'm sorry for forgetting to do nice things. You two and Jean, I feel like I've just left you all out of my life lately."

Olive and Bailey looked at each other. In unison, they both said, "It's not all about you, Jane." and then they giggled. They giggled at me, the poor sick person in the bed.

I crossed my arms and said, "Well, I'm the one lying in this bed right now, and that DOES make it about me, so there."

There was no ready comeback for that, so I chalked it up for a win on my part.

"So, why am I in bed? I don't feel particularly sick, just kind of weird."

They exchanged glances.

"What? What is it that I don't know about?"

Olive said, "Well, you almost had an accident."

"An accident?"

"Uh huh. You woke up long enough to tell me you had the strangest dream, and then you passed out again until just now. Why don't you tell us about the dream and then we'll tell you about the accident."

I thought about it. "Well, I went to visit a couple people in Paris, and one in Beaulieu-sur-mer, and then I went to Lyon and visited another person." I frowned. "It's a very detailed dream, isn't it? And in fact, at least part of it isn't a dream. I mean, I met the detective guy in Paris before I ever left."

About then it all came back to me.

"Oh crap, it wasn't a dream, was it? That poor girl. And ..."

I looked at Olive. "You saved me, didn't you? And I bet you didn't tell Bailey."

Bailey was looking at Olive oddly. "What aren't you telling me?"

And at me, "What d'you mean, saved you?"

"It's all still kind of dreamy, but I'm fairly sure I took a dive off a building in Lyon and Olive appeared in the elevator and saved me. Olive?"

"Well, did you expect me to just let you fall?"

Softly, "No, of course not. But I thought you were in therapy."

"I was. I'd just been released a few hours before that."

Bailey was looking back and forth like that tennis match you hear about. "What? Why don't I know anything about any of this? What happened?"

"Bailey, I did leave you voicemails."

"I didn't get them until ... well, later. I was busy. And you left a ridiculous number of them. And Olive was being Olive." She finally ran down.

"Look, there's nothing wrong with me that sleep didn't fix. Or actually, there probably is something wrong with me, but I hope Olive can fix it. Anyhow, get out of the way, I'm taking a shower and after that, I'm having a nice cup of tea loaded up with sugar, and then some pancakes and bacon ..."

My phone started ringing. I sighed. "It's gonna be one of those days, I can tell."

I got on the phone and started talking, mostly listening, took some notes and then hung up.

"I'm still taking my shower. I'll talk with you two when I get out. Meanwhile, tea and pancakes, tout de suite!"

I went in the bathroom, then stuck my head back out again, rolling my hand, "That means, right away! Capisce?"

Olive said, with a smirk, "I hear and obey, my liege."

Bailey snickered. "Yeah, my liege."

I said, in a grand tone, "See that you do, my minions." I shook my head. No respect.

The big advantage to it being an apartment instead of just a hotel room was that it has an enormous shower, and a fancy

The Evershaw Curse

showerhead. It felt so luxurious taking a long, hot shower, so relaxing. I had no idea how tense I was. Although, I was thinking back on all that and I knew that most of it had been false feelings, generated by whatever it was. Of course, it was helped along by the whole jetlag thing, and worry about Olive.

I got out of the shower, toweled all off and got my hair in some semblance of order. I put on fresh undies and fresh clothes and felt like a fresh me. Brushed teeth and a little makeup and I was set to face the world.

I exited the bathroom to heavenly smells. It appeared that Olive had stocked the apartment just as I suspected, as there was bacon, eggs and pancakes waiting. And heavenly tea. I should just forget Dale and marry these two. I told them so, and they snickered.

Bailey remarked, "We already have other plans, Jane. So just forget about having galley slaves the rest of your life!"

"Life is so hard, and you can't get good help."

We all sat down and had breakfast, or lunch, or whatever the heck this was, and I talked. I told them about the detective in Paris, Luc in Beaulieu-sur-mer. I filled them in on what had happened in Lyon, including my exit from the rooftops.

Olive got out her sonic screwdriver and scanned me, but she said it was kind of inconclusive, that her little gadget didn't have the power to really do much with this sort of thing and she'd want to turn it over to Jean. Which was a major admission for Olive, in my eyes, and showed how much she'd changed. Thank goodness it was an internal change, and she'd kept her attitude, though. I'd have been hard pressed to think it an improvement if she'd lost her snark.

Then I turned to the phone call.

"The girl's name is Juliette, and she's one of the two people that were involved the night that Bart vanished. You probably remember that she and Jon-Paul were the two hotel staff that got fired over his disappearance because they were dilly-dallying while on work hours."

Bailey snickered. "Did you actually say 'dilly-dallying', Jane?"

"Yes, I did. So there. Anyhow, before I was so rudely interrupted, I was talking about Juliette. It turns out that her boyfriend at the time went bungee jumping a few days later and wound up dying of it. And now, probably since I brought it all back to her mind again, she's tried to kill herself - they pumped a whole crapload of pills out of her stomach. They think she's going to make it, though."

I stopped and sipped some tea. "I'm beginning to think of this as the curse of the Evershaws. Or I would, but of course, being that Olive is all sciency and has all kinds of interesting powers, I tend to think of it more in that light. Don't you think it's all just pretty suspicious, all these deaths associated with Bart and Naomi? And the weird thing is, it seems like it's still happening. Like someone continues to cover up Bart vanishing. And why in the world would they do that?"

Bailey mused, "I wonder if Naomi knows anything."

I shook my head. "I don't think she does. But why is she still alive if someone's trying so hard to keep Bart's disappearance from being solved? I mean, wouldn't the easiest thing to do be to just 'disappear' Naomi as well? Especially since it seems like she must be a real thorn in someone's side."

I took a breath. "Guys, I was so slow. I was so dragged down. By the time I got to Juliette's apartment, it was all I could do to pull myself up the stairs to her house. I mean, I run up a Stairmaster hundreds of reps with no problem. How could taking the stairs at her house be any big deal? And yet, I was so gone that I nearly stopped halfway up the first flight."

Olive said, "When did you first start feeling this way, Jane?"

"Well, I was trying to think back, and it really seems like it was when I got to Paris. I remember being so messed up by the jetlag that I really needed some extra sleep and desperately wanted to just take a long nap. I thought it was the jetlag, but what if part of it was me getting this ... whatever it is settled into me? But I didn't meet anyone in Paris until I'd been there for a while. Of course, I guess it could have been jetlag, and then it became something else after I met with Renaud Amach at the detective agency. You suppose he could have given me something, or fed me something?"

Bailey threw in, "I thought you said he was a nice guy."

"Well, yeah, but nice guys do bad things sometimes. And he did spend a lot of time trying to talk me out of taking the case."

Olive shook her head. "I don't think it's him. I did some research, and he's right. There have been some strange deaths. I looked back over Naomi's data and then cross checked with death stats for those years. It pretty much seems like anyone that did any serious work on Bart's disappearance had something happen to them."

I said, "Like what?"

"Well, it's hard to really say, since some people like Luc and the Jon-Rene guy just suddenly retired, and that's hard to track unless you know them. But most of them just got really unlucky. There's one from Florida, by the way. He got back from France and while he was at the airport, he managed to jump into a jet engine. Ruined the engine."

I made a face, "Must have ruined the guy."

"Yeah, that too."

"That sounds like one of the ones Renaud mentioned that went off and did the case anyway after he warned them. Kind of like I did. And I almost wound up like they did - dead of an accident."

Bailey nodded. "Doesn't sound like an accident anymore, does it?"

"Nope."

We all sat there contemplating our navels.

"Olive, did all the people who died or were incapacitated come to Paris first? Or maybe more easily, did anyone who died, not come to Paris first?"

"Either way, it doesn't seem so. I mean, there were a couple deaths associated with this case that probably aren't associated with this case. I mean, deaths that look like just 'normal' deaths."

I nodded. "It's hard to accept that something unknown is doing something subtle enough that we have to talk about this like it's … normal. Normal deaths vs not-normal deaths. I feel like an insurance actuary."

Bailey said, "Not to inject anything unscientific into this conversation, but … er … is it possible that it IS some sort of Egyptian curse or something?" She looked at Olive. "Well? Is that even possible?"

"Why you lookin' at me?"

"Because you have all the knowledge in the world in that little pea brain of yours."

Olive smiled. "In my research I found that people have to really like you before they'll insult you, since they have to have faith that you know that they don't mean it."

Bailey stared at her. "How much work did it take to make a sentence like that? Weeks of study?"

Olive grinned at me. "No, just listening to Jane a lot."

"That'll do it."

I said, "Hey! Enough of that. Bruised ego here."

They both hugged me, and Bailey said, "Jane, you don't have any ego to bruise. But we love you anyhow." That made me smile, and I felt better.

Olive said, "But to answer your question, probably not, Bailey. The thing about it is though, from purely empirical data, it almost seems possible that psychic things actually do happen. But as a purely scientific being, I can't address their reality."

Bailey rolled her eyes, "So, you're useless."

Olive nodded. "Yeah, I guess so."

Bailey hugged her and said, "Well, I'm not mad at you anymore. But don't push it. I still have to work on James and find out if it was YOU or just him being him that made him interested."

Olive slugged Bailey on the shoulder and said, "It wasn't me - didya ever consider the idea that it might actually be YOU, Bailey? Yer pretty cute and sexy for an old broad."

"You just had to add that last part, didn't you?"

"Just trying to be honest."

"Don't try so hard."

It was great hearing them back arguing again. Music to my ears.

Chapter Twenty-Five

I See You.

After the haranguing came to an end, I magicked up an Uber, and we went down and waited for it to arrive.

I finally got a chance to really look, and said, "Olive, you look adorable in your little kids' version of the Mariners outfit. Did you get that yourself?"

Olive sneered at Bailey, "No, my dearest friend picked it out for me. I'm also wearing your underwear, but since it was all new, I figured I was safe."

"Oh. Good to know."

That got me set to thinking about other things as well, wondering just how far Olive had gone. As far as I could tell, she was all natural. Sooo…

"Stop thinking Jane, you're gonna hurt yourself."

In my own defense, I said, "Hey, I have to admit I've never known for sure if you … like… formed clothes or if you bought them."

"Oh. I thought you were thinking of other stuff. Yeah, I buy everything. Same deal as the water jug, remember? Where it wasn't worth the energy cost to make water? Same with clothes. Not to say I couldn't do it if I needed to, but I'll stay with just doing the hair and calling it good."

Which brought that same subject back up, but the Uber arrived in time to keep me from sticking my foot in my mouth.

Olive grinned at me, though, so I know that she knew what I was thinking.

The Uber driver was a big burly no-nonsense kinda guy. He also didn't seem to have any interest in hauling three cute girls, beyond simply getting from point A to point B, so we all stayed quiet and it was a fairly short, very quiet ride.

He pulled up in front of the Lyon Sud hospital and we piled out, and he drove off, all pretty much without a word. We all looked at each other and laughed.

Olive said, "His loss."

Bailey said, "I don't think he's interested much in girls."

I chimed in with, "Or at least not these girls."

We made our way up to the entrance of the hospital. Hospitals seem to be pretty much the same building all over the world. I mean, big and white and lots of floor space with lots of people running around like they know what they're doing. Which I very much hope they do. I know they've put me back together a few times. I reflected on that for a minute, glancing at Olive and thinking about how I probably wouldn't have needed any hospitalization without her. It would have been straight to the morgue. A happy thought.

She smiled at me and patted my shoulder, and I smiled back. It's great to have friends. Especially friends who can save you from the consequences of diving off the side of a building. From 4000 miles away. Although, I suppose that particular set of circumstances is fairly rare.

We arrived at the front desk. Thank goodness there was a placard that said, "English this queue."

I stepped up and said, "Hi, I'm Jane Bond. I'd like to see Juliette Duvine?"

He looked up the patient records and said, "What is your relationship with the patient?"

"I don't really have a relationship, but I was the one who called the emergency for her."

That seemed to make it ok for him, and he said, "You're actually in luck. She's been transferred from ICU to a regular room." He pointed along the hallway, "Follow the yellow line to the elevators, she's on the sixth floor, room 6121. Check in with the nurse's station up there, your friends won't be able to go in with you."

"Thank you!" I smiled at him and he smiled back. Nice guy.

So we followed the yellow line. It was pretty quick to the elevator, and then pretty quick up to the sixth floor. We exited the elevator and looked around. Down the hall a little way was an unmistakable nurse's station. Like I say, everything looks the same in a hospital. Then we ran into a snag. The English-speaking person was on a break, apparently. I said, "Let's just sit and wait." since my experience with my French was that it was better to not say anything.

Then, of course, Olive spoke up and started spouting flowery French phrases, and the girl at the desk was all smiles. The girl pointed down the hallway back the way we'd come and smiled especially brightly at Olive.

Olive said, "I might have a date."

I rolled my eyes. "What about Juliette?"

"Oh, her. Yeah, she's down this way. Aluette said we could all go in as long as we're quiet."

"Aluette? Like the song?"

"Uh huh. Cute, huh?"

I bet she hates it as much as I did being Jane Bond.

We headed down the hallway and found room 6121. A gentle knock and we entered.

The girl lying in the bed was very pale, and her blonde hair looked like it was in need of a wash. I guess they don't worry much about those things when they bring someone in that needs their stomach pumped. As we entered, her eyes opened, and I got the impression of a scared woodland bunny in her gaze. Bailey and Olive picked up on it right away and scattered to the chairs, where they might be out of the way and less of a threat.

"Hi, Juliette."

"Who are you?"

"Oh, you speak English. I'm so glad."

"Oui, I speak the good English, I am working with tourists a lot. But who are you?"

"My name is Jane Bond. I came to visit you and found you … sick."

She grimaced. "Yes, I was sick. Mon dieu, I wish you had not found me. Why did you have to come along?"

I was at a loss for words. "I thought …"

"I know what you thought, you Americans come and think you know everything. Well I say to you, next time you do not do me favors, please."

"Next time?"

She looked at me balefully, if a rabbit can be said to have a baleful look. "Oui. It is too hard, being like me. My life is bad. I am so tired of being scared and alone."

She dashed at the tears in her eyes. "I will try again and again, and I will be successful. You cannot stop me no matter how you try."

"Juliette, I don't understand. I talked with you on the phone, you sounded like you were willing to talk with me about Bart's disappearance."

She seemed to shrink in on herself a little. "That is true, I did. But then, after I talked with you, all those things came back. And Jon-Paul." She gave a little cry. "Jon-Paul is still gone. You cannot bring him back. And I cannot go forward without him."

The poor girl looked more like a sad rabbit the more she said. Tears were slowly forming, but it was like there were no more tears, no matter how much she wanted to shed them. It made me all the more angry at this ... person ... who would wantonly break someone and leave them to suffer. And finally die.

Olive touched my arm, and I looked at her. She looked queasy, but she said, "I can help her a little bit. I can't fix her, but I think I can help the worst of her fear."

"Are you sure you can do this?"

"I can do it, but only because it's something for you, something for her. Not something for me. Do you see?"

I nodded. "I see. Well, she's so sad. If you can straighten out a little of what was done, maybe it will help until we find the proper way to fix things. It makes ME feel selfish, though, since this is more for me than for her."

"In the end, it's all for her, Jane."

I nodded and Olive got out her 'sonic screwdriver'. She surreptitiously pointed it in the general direction of Juliette's head for a few seconds, then hugged me and sat back down.

I looked at Juliette, caught her eye. "I know it seems that sometimes there's no way to move forward, but from my experience, there's always some direction you can go. There's always some path. It may be hard to see, but it's always there."

Juliette's hopelessness didn't seem to be quite as pronounced, but she said, "It is all black ahead though, Ms. Bond. I cannot see anything that looks like a way out."

"What did you and Jon-Paul talk about, Juliette? What did you think of for a future?"

Her face softened a little, and she said, "Jon was always looking for the way out, like you say. He always had a plan, always had a path. He was so … it was like he was a high flyer and he could see what was happening ahead. It was strange though, Ms. Bond. At the last, he was turning more and more into a daredevil. He would throw himself into the most dangerous things, always looking for a scare. I had to work and work even to get him to attach a bungee cord to him that day. He thought he could escape an accident even without a cord. I was worried about him then, that something was wrong. That something had changed. But I was also changed. After he was gone, and he wasn't there to help me see the way forward, I stopped caring about it. I've been sitting waiting for something to kill me ever since the day he died. It just seemed to me that I had nothing but that to look forward to. And it would be the only way I'd ever see my Jon again."

I bent over her bed and kissed her forehead. "Give me a chance, Juliette. Let me try to find a way to help you to feel better. Promise me you won't try again right away to leave this earth behind."

She looked deep into my eyes and finally she nodded. "I will endure a while longer, Jane Bond. But do not forget me too long. I want to join my Jon."

There seemed nothing more we could add, so we all trooped out and back down the corridor. Olive winked at the reception girl as we passed, and she simpered and waved.

"You really do have a date with her, don't you, Olive?"

She smirked at me. "Sure seems like it, don't it?"

Chapter Twenty-Six

Cabbages and kings, and sealing wax ...

We decided that since it didn't appear that anyone had any real interest in talking to me, and that since we could now just jump back to the apartment if we needed to show up anyplace in a cab, that we'd go home to Chelan and spend some quality time examining my brain. Jean was looking forward to it, as a matter of fact. For my part, it wasn't the sort of thing I was very happy about, but I was definitely the most available guinea pig. After seeing poor Juliette, I was willing to do about anything if we could figure out how to fix her. Or at least keep her from suiciding as soon as she decided she'd waited long enough.

A few minutes later, we were looking out at the familiar walls of Kit's giant garage, and a few minutes after that, I was sitting at my favorite place - the little nook in the kitchen. I think most of the darkness I'm remembering from the past several days is from internal issues, but it was wonderful to see the Chelan sun smiling down on me. We'd reset the clock the other way this time, and here it was early morning. Which meant we could have breakfast again! I know, I come off a little obsessed with breakfast, but it's a meal with lots of potential.

I could actually feel the blackness swirling around me, like I was in the center of some kind of psychic tornado, but at least for now I had the sun and my friends.

Jean joined us for breakfast. I could tell that she'd been practicing, since she handled everything about breakfast with ease. She didn't make any pancakes or waffles, but she was watching Olive while Olive flipped the pancakes, and I could see a gleam of interest there.

Midway through breakfast, Jean piped up, "Oh, I forgot! Bailey, there's someone here to see you. He's been sitting outside in his car for over 37 hours. I have allowed him access to the restroom facilities in the garage, I hope that's all right."

Bailey said, "He who?" She set her mouth. "I don't know any he's."

Jean said, "Oh my, I should have checked in before I allowed him to have access to the household."

I shook my head, "Bailey. Is this James? Because if it is, I think you at least owe him a chance. He's been outside for nearly two days."

Olive helpfully projected the car from outside the house on a big screen in the kitchen. We all looked at him.

Olive said, "He's cuter than I remember."

Bailey snapped at Olive, "He's mine. Don't touch."

Olive grinned. "Go get 'im, tiger."

I said, "Hey, guys - how did we get here? If we haven't been here in the last two days, how did we suddenly appear?"

Grudgingly, Olive said, "Ok, I'll get the car and we'll drive up the driveway. If he sees Jane in the house, he'll be so besotted with Bailey that he won't think about it anyway. I'll drop Bailey off at his car, and then park up at the garage."

It sounded like a plan, so the two of them exited down the stairs. That left me alone with Jean. I looked at her and said, "Well, are we ready for this? What should I do?"

She smiled and said, "You can just sit there, Jane. I have scans going and have since you got here. We should be able to get to the bottom of this. Or actually, we WILL be able to. I'm very confident we can not only fix the issue that came to you, but we can also make you proof against it happening again. However, a lot of that is because the nano-devices you have in your body are providing something of a firewall. For any normal human, we may not be able to reverse the damage."

With only a trace of bitterness, I said, "Normal human."

Gravely, she said, "Yes, normal human. Jane, you are no longer a 'normal human' and for better or worse when Olive made this change to you, I find that I cannot remove it without express orders from Jane Bond to do so."

I breathed out a long sigh. "So, I could actually ask you to remove the nanobots and you would have to do so?"

There was a long hesitation, but finally Jean said, "Yes. I could remove the nanobots. Do you understand why it would be such a hard decision for myself or another artificial to make, though?"

"I suppose. It would mean that the Jane Bond organism would not live as long or as well, and therefore would be potentially detrimental to the Jane Bond organism to have them removed."

Jean stilled a moment and looked at me. "Sarcasm aside, I do see that you understand the issue, Lady Bond. You can look at it as an inconvenience, something you can make a decision about if you wish. But to Olive and even more, to myself, it is not something to play games with. It is deadly serious in a game where Jane Bond is of the utmost importance in all decisions."

I tried to laugh about it, I said, "So, it IS all about me."

Jean ruined it completely by saying, "Yes, it is."

What answer could I give to that? Indeed, did I really want the nanos removed from my body? And in the end, did I want to see about having them 'installed' in Bailey? And in Georgia? Dale? Perhaps James at some point? At what point does it stop? But at what point could I fail to do it? Would I still look 30 as Georgia was dying of old age?

Going the other way, though, when I reached 60 or 70 years of age and the nanos had been removed today, would I be as willing to let life go if I had a chance to keep it? Or would I be strong enough to pass on as all my ancestors had, simply living as long a life as was intended.

Jean interrupted my internal monologue, saying, "I believe we have found it. It's a very ingenious bit of organic code inserted into your system. It was … it appears to have been grown there. Like a 'seed' was planted, and as it grows, it takes over more and more of your system. In your case, the 'seed' is 'fed' from a desire to work on the Evershaw case. The more you work on the case, the larger and hardier, and more virulent the code becomes. At some point it is impossible to stop and impossible to subvert. Luc Cardone has kept it under control for years in some unconscious way by never thinking or talking of police work. He may now be in jeopardy if he cannot stop himself from thinking about this case."

"The seed is custom created for each person, it appears. It draws upon natural tendencies such as desire to find the solution in your case and in Luc Cardone's. In the case of Juliette, I feel it grew initially since there was so much attention paid to Bart's disappearance. Juliette's natural tendency to be non-confrontational and solitary was magnified. Jon-Paul's tendency toward aspiring to new heights, new challenges, new paths was magnified. Unfortunately, Jon-Paul's path was cut short by too much aspiration."

"Your nanobots have been programmed to find and destroy this organism, and it is indeed an organism with even a rudimentary intelligence, at least enough to tailor itself to the environment in which it finds itself. It's quite a find. I will incorporate this into our future studies."

My mind blanked on some of what Jean had said, but I picked up the part about 'find and destroy'. "I'm cured?"

"Well, cured isn't really the word so much as disinfected, or perhaps sprayed for termites."

There was definitely humor in her tone, and I felt that Jean was becoming a real person.

"So, can we help Juliette and Luc?"

"I believe so, Lady Bond. We can create a special set of nanobots that will seek out the organism and remove it. Once it is removed, the nanobots will shut down so nothing will remain of them and no future changes will be made."

"Oh Jean, that's stellar!"

I could hear a blush in her voice as she said, "Why, thank you, Lady Bond."

"How would we administer this to them?"

"I believe the best way would be to send a card to them, and inside it, have an unusually pleasant scent that they will sniff into their nasal passages. The nanobots will be installed by that intake of breath."

The thought of that gave me a shiver, considering how easy it would be to infect the entire world with something like that.

"Jean, nothing like this could be done without my express permission, or perhaps even orders, correct?"

"I can make that so, Jane Bond."

The Evershaw Curse

"Please, make it so. "

"It is done, Jane Bond."

I sighed again, a regular occurrence these days. It seemed the deeper I swam, the deeper the lake got.

Chapter Twenty-Seven

Reconciliations

Olive drove up the little hill toward Jane's house, making the hairpin turns that so frustrated crane drivers and delighted sports car aficionados. Her little Saturn Sky took the curves with aplomb, and Olive was over the moon when she pulled up next to the rental car in Jane's driveway. She had a sudden thought.

"Bailey, I just thought of something."

Bailey snarked, "Did it hurt?"

"Yeah, some. But I'm serious. When did you meet Carstead the first time? I mean, this time, not the first first time."

Bailey rolled her eyes and said, "You really have been talking to Jane too much. But, it was that weekend we all went out. Jane had that thing up at Georgia's house, and I went to Vegas." She frowned. "Was that when you voodoo'd Carstead?"

Olive shook her head slowly. "No, that's what I just was thinking. I was in Portland that weekend that we all took off."

Bailey frowned. "But…"

"Yea, but. I was in Portland when you went to Vegas. I went to Vegas the next week, remember, when we started investigating. You went to New Jersey."

"Don't remind me."

"Bailey, I'm being serious here. I didn't 'mess with' Carstead's head until you went to Jersey. You met up with Carstead before I ever even saw him. I'd never met him before, remember?"

Bailey glanced over at Olive. "So, you never met him before I saw him that weekend."

"Nope. I just stopped in at the MGM while I was in Vegas talking to one of the UFO guys. I figured I'd sneak by Carstead just to prove that I'm smarter than him."

Bailey gave her a lopsided smile. "And you're not?"

"Well, yeah, I'm still smarter than him. But he got me on that one."

"So, he um … he liked me before you even met him."

Olive nodded.

Bailey gave her a big smile and a hug. "He likes me."

Olive nodded again. "Yeah, I think so. Although you have to admit that fifteen planters full of roses and camping in our driveway – I think it's more than just like."

She pushed Bailey out and then motored on up to the garage.

Bailey crept up to the car and looked through the slightly foggy window. James was in an extremely uncomfortable position, and it looked like his neck was going to feel broken when he woke. She'd been feeling particularly benevolent toward him even before Olive had her lightning bolt thought.

Like Olive said, they had come up the driveway and found scattered every so often along the road, fifteen planters with roses in them, a different color rose for every planter.

To top it off, James sitting cramped in the car looked just a little too adorkable for words.

She quietly tried the passenger door and managed to get into the car without waking him. He smelled good, even after camping in the car for two days, and she'd have to thank Jean for letting him use the facilities. She leaned over the console and snuggled up to him.

He woke with a jerk, a gasp of breath, and another of pain when his neck realized what position he'd been in for hours. It took about three seconds for comprehension to come into his eyes, and when it did, they lit up like candles.

"Bailey", he whispered.

"Hi. Got your flowers. Never found the card."

He gave her a James smile. "I'm the card."

"Ah, I see. Saving on postage and natural resources. Very smart."

He nodded, awake enough to be a little alarmed. "I expected to be looking at a gun or at least a baseball bat."

The Evershaw Curse

She smirked. "I can get one, if it's what you need."

"Oh no, no, I'm fine. I'll make do with… " He caressed her face. "You're really here. I thought I might never see you again."

She gave him back his halfway grin and said, "No, you're not that lucky, James."

He kissed her and said, "Oh, I think I'm very lucky."

Of one accord, they got out of the car and Bailey led him up the steps and inside, where they waved at Jean, Jane and Olive. Then they went down the stairs to Bailey's room and apologized to each other. Several times.

Chapter Twenty-Eight

Recriminations

We all sat at the big dining room table, me and Olive, Bailey and Jean. We had found we were out of wine and nacho chips, so James had 'volunteered' to go get some fresh stocks.

Of course, this was nothing to do with food, for once.

"So, we have so much data it should be easy to find the source of the problem, and I'd be willing to bet, the location of either Bart, or at least Bart's body."

Bailey was eating leftover bacon from breakfast and the chips that we were unable to find so James could run his errand. I was having some bits of candy that looked like they were left from last year's Halloween celebration. You know how that is, there's always something in the random selection that no one likes and it's still there hanging around the house for those desperate days. Everyone else had a variety of whatever they'd found, and we actually were looking forward to having James back, since whatever he brought with him had to be better than what we had.

Bailey said, "Maybe. I mean, the problem we have is that we have people spread all over the world, really. I guess almost all of them are either in France or the US, but how do we know?"

"Well, I think if we analyze the data points, we can come up with an answer."

"That sounds very professional, Jane. Where did you read that?"

"Bathroom wall, probably."

We all snickered.

"But, seriously folks, we have data spread all over the world, but in the end, we only have dead bodies there in France. The two bits we have in the US are the only ones we found, and they are definitely from an 'infection' point of France."

Jean said, "Don't call it an infection point, that's bad optics."

"Heh. Jean, you've been watching too much politics. Bad optics or not though, it is what it is. We have to think in terms of infection point, since we have to find out where the problem stems from. Now, since we can rule out the US and concentrate on France, that makes it a lot easier. And really, in France, about the only things we have to consider are Paris, Lyon and Beaulieu-Sur-Mer.

Olive kicked in, "And the marrow farmer in Belgium."

I nodded. "I guess, but that basically says that we can ignore him, and Luc in Beaulieu and Juliette in Lyon. I mean, they're all people that got infected in Paris and left to go someplace else. That reminds me, Jean, can you send our marrow farmer a gift as well?"

She gave me a thumbs up. "On it, Boss."

I'm really liking this new Jean.

We kicked that back and forth for a few minutes and suddenly it hit me.

"Guys, we keep saying Paris, Lyon and Beaulieu, but what are we missing."

Bailey frowned, "Missing what?"

"Think about it a minute. What are we missing?"

They all racked their brains, and no one came up with anything. "Is this one of those obvious things that's just going to make us angry when we figure it out?"

I replied, "Probably. Give up?"

There were mutinous mutterings, but finally they all said, "Yeah, we give up. What are we missing?"

I said, "Esternay."

Silence.

"What's Esternay?"

"It's the city that Essie lives in."

Silence again.

Then, "But how did we not include that?"

I frowned. "I'm not sure, but we did go there twice. We never went back to check on the body though, Olive."

She shivered and said, "I have no wish to see that again, I'm not sure why it bothered me so much, though."

Bailey said, "But why is it any different from any other person that left Paris? Essie left Paris, too."

I leaned back and crossed my arms. "I'm not really sure why. But for some reason it feels like we should follow up on it. Maybe because she was the first person I interviewed, I feel like I might have missed something. And remember, she had a different story than the two drunk guys did."

Olive said, "Yeah, and she also didn't seem to be affected by it. By the 'infection' since as far as you said to us anyhow, she seemed to be a completely normal, old retired lady."

I ran my hand over my forehead, tired of this not knowing things. "I know, and for that matter, Luc seems normal too. Of course, it only took me about ten minutes of talking to Luc before I understood what his problem was. Fear of detecting. Our two guys in the US had drinking issues in weird ways. Cluzet took a dive into the ground and was even thinking about not using a bungee cord. Three weird suicides from the detective agency in Paris, and his mention of at least two more that really stick out. I mean, how many people suicide by diving into a running jet engine?"

I looked up at them all. "And, of course, me. I have to put myself into the mix, since without Olive's quick reflexes and amazing thought processes, I wouldn't be here right now."

I smiled fondly at Olive, then mused, "And I wasn't in Paris the night it happened, all the rest of them were. Except the Paris detectives. Jean, can you run a check and see if our data includes information regarding whether the dead detectives went to see Essie?"

"It does, Jane. And of the eight detectives that appear to be affected, seven of them went to see Essie first. The remaining one did not file a report before he was killed in a traffic accident. I suspect he went to see Essie and was very susceptible to whatever was given him."

I thought about it. "Jean, I only count six detectives. What are the additional two you came up with?"

"Lady Bond, I cross-analyzed the data to pick up American detective agencies. My data is not comprehensive, but it appears that two of the agencies sent detectives in person. Both of those detectives were involved in accidental-seeming deaths. Although, hanging yourself in your hotel room in Esternay seems difficult to resolve as accidental."

"Wow. And if the rest of the American agencies called Renaud Amach first, they likely would have been warned off, or possibly called Essie or one of the drunks on the phone and decided it wasn't worth the trouble for what Naomi could afford to pay."

I made a face. "If we were charging Naomi for what we've done so far, she'd be paying us the rest of her life. I haven't tracked any of it since I have no intention of charging her more than a token amount, but it's no wonder that no one was willing to find him with all the roadblocks in the way."

"Roadblocks that might have been put there by Essie."

About then, I heard the gravel crunch in the driveway outside and said, "Let's finish this up since that sounds like James has returned with food. Olive and I will head back to Esternay tomorrow to check in with Essie and see what we can find out. I suspect she'll be a hard nut to crack."

A shout from the driveway made me smile, "Hey, all you lazy people in there, come help me carry stuff!"

It sounded like James was already fitting in. We all piled out into the driveway and James had done himself proud. He looked to have bought out Safeway. It seemed we'd be having a very snackilicious dinner.

V.R. Tapscott

Chapter Twenty-Nine

Recidivism

Olive and I decided we'd hit the newspaper office in Esternay before we went looking for evidence that Essie was our culprit. To that end, we elevator'd into a small pizza place. Esternay doesn't have a lot of businesses, but we figured that would be one of the easiest places if we landed in the restroom. It was an exceedingly small restroom and quite a squeeze for Olive to get the elevator in, but she got it and we still managed to get out of the room. Something we should have thought about earlier was that in a very small restaurant it would be hard to escape notice, since how did we come out of the restroom if no one saw us go in? Needless to say, we garnered some curious looks, but everyone seems to be able to make their own peace with impossible things before breakfast. Or well after breakfast, considering we'd had to leave Chelan at about 6am to be able to have any time at all in France. This time difference was annoying! And yes, we have decided it's all about me.

The Evershaw Curse

At any rate, we had some nice breakfast pizza, or at least that's what I told myself. Pizza crust, bacon and cheese is pretty close to the same thing as a McDonald's sandwich, right? I thought about asking to have an egg on our pizza but thought maybe that would be pushing it too far, plus I suppose pizza places would have no reason to have eggs.

We sat munching on our lunch, considering our next move, which would be finding old newspapers. Maybe at a library or newspaper office. Or considering the entertainment quotient in Esternay, they might have last week's paper right here in the pizza place!

I had just come up with this gem of an idea when Olive poked me and pointed out the window. She got the seat facing the window, and she'd been watching people go by.

I turned and looked. I turned back. "What?"

She frowned and said, "By the store window across the street. Look!"

I did, and this time I saw it. I boggled. "But he's ... he's dead!"

The guy from Essie's house was there, across the street, munching on a hot dog or whatever they eat in Esternay. Maybe pizza.

I turned back to Olive and said, "You said he was dead. He'd been dead thirteen hours or something."

Olive blushed a little. "If you remember, I said I was joking about the time of death and what he'd eaten and stuff."

I whispered furiously, "But he was dead, right? That was the salient point of the question!"

"Yes, yes, he was dead. I think."

I glared at her. "What do you mean, 'you think'??"

"Well, he didn't have a pulse, and I didn't get any brain activity."

My eyebrows went up, "That sounds pretty freekin' dead to me! Why is he out there walking around eating stuff that will kill him in a few years?"

"It could be carrots, I can't tell from here."

I didn't say anything. Loudly.

"Well, um. See… "

She seemed to be hung up on something. I ahem'd at her.

"All right, I don't know, see? I told you I'm a pilot, not a doctor! He looked dead, he acted dead, he smelled dead. Maybe he was just asleep. It scared the crap out of me, as you remember. I played dead for a while myself!"

I crossed my arms, then discovered I couldn't eat my pizza that way and uncrossed them. I finished the pizza.

"Ok, what's he doing now."

"He's just standing there."

I gathered my wrappers and drummed my fingers. "What about now?"

"He finished his food and wiped his hands on his pants. Now he's looking in the shop. Oh, hey…"

"Hey what?"

"It's a gun shop."

"Essie likes to trap-shoot. He probably is buying ammo. Or target thingies."

We waited a little, I drank my pop, Olive sucked down some more tomato juice.

"He's just standing there."

After a bit, "Essie just came out with a sack. Pretty heavy, you were probably right. She handed it to him to carry. Think we should follow them?"

"Maybe let them get home, then check in on him. It's not like we don't know where he lives. So to speak."

So, we sat there a while longer. I had some more pop. I wasn't exactly upset at Olive, but it was a close race. I mean, is the guy dead or not? Should be pretty obvious, I'd think. Of course, I hadn't bothered to reach out and check for a pulse either, and then someone had been banging on the door and we'd all run for it.

We got up from our table, tipped and smiled our way out the front door (which we'd never come in) and stopped at the sidewalk. Essie's house was only about half a mile from there, so we started walking. I wasn't sure how fast the guy would have been walking, especially if he was dead for a while. It might take it out of you, y'know? I'd been near enough to death enough times to tell you, if that was any indication, being dead would slow you down a lot.

So, we walked kinda slowly along, looking at the landscape.

"Whatta we gonna do when we get there?"

I shrugged. "I figured we'd sneak up and play it by ear. Maybe Essie's out target-shooting."

We arrived at the cowshed and snuck around the back side, planning on scoping out the area and then seeing what was going on with mister dead guy. However, about the time we came even with the back of the house, we heard a gunshot. I figured that Essie was shooting again, but when we stuck our heads around the corner, there was the dead guy holding a gun on Essie and she was kind of laying limply over to one side, an obvious spread of blood under her.

I jumped around the corner and yelled, "Drop your gun!"

I have no idea to this day why I thought he'd pay any attention to me since I didn't have a gun or a badge or a bad attitude, even. And he didn't. Or at least he didn't drop his gun. Instead, with a hunted look on his face, he wheeled on me and fired off a shot.

My left shoulder lit up on fire, and I gasped. Olive made a noise like a mad bull and pointed her sonic screwdriver at the formerly dead guy. He dropped.

She turned to me. "Are you ok? What happened?"

"He shot me, that's what happened! Ow. I think it's just a crease though, it's hardly bleeding. What about Essie?"

I yanked off a chunk of my shirt and stuffed it up under the shoulder to keep the blood mostly inside me.

We made it to Essie's side, and I got down on my knees. She was sitting kind of sideways with a lot of blood spreading from a wound in her chest, but it didn't look like it was fatal, probably just hurt like hell.

What she whispered was the most surprising, though. "He's an alien, he's held me captive for years. Don't let him get away!" Then, as if she'd been holding on by a thread, she passed out. She still had a pulse, so it looked like she was at least alive. I ripped off a section of her shirt and pressed it against where the blood was coming from.

I looked at Olive. Unexpected, this is.

It was weird to be doing it, but I felt around Essie's clothes until I found her phone. I pulled it out, and trying to sound like anyone but me, I called 112 for the second time in three days and reported my reason for calling. They assured me they'd have someone on the way as soon as they could. And yes, I used a piece of cloth for fingerprints. Sheesh.

I looked at Essie and the alien. "Crap. Olive, can we elevator the alien to Chelan and have Jean work on him? I mean, we're not giving him over to the police anyhow, right? We can't just hand over an alien."

I thought about it further. "Olive, do you think Essie saw you?"

Olive thought about it, which I suppose meant she was reviewing whatever movie I assume she keeps of her life. I'll have to ask about that.

Anyhow, she said, "I don't think she could have seen me, she had her eyes closed, and I didn't go near her."

I nodded. "Ok. The nanobots will fix my bullet hole, right? And assuming they can, really fast, will you grab me a shirt?"

She gave me a thumbs up, and even as she left I could feel the wound stop hurting, and she vanished. Seconds later, she reappeared with a shirt. I grabbed off the shirt I was wearing and spit on the tail, or what was left of it, and wiped the blood away from my shoulder. The wound had already stopped bleeding and was starting to look less and less like anything but a scratch. I slipped the new shirt on, tossed the old one into the elevator, and we both picked up mister Alien and got him inside. We also grabbed the gun. Nothing else seemed to be out of place.

I'd figured on waiting for the cops to get there, but chickened out. Being at two crime scenes in succession would be kind of suspicious. Heck, even I thought it was suspicious.

"Let's go!" I said. I could hear sirens in the distance. I looked back at Essie, but figured any second now she'd have more help than I could give, anyhow.

About then, Olive's eyes went wide. "Jane, he hasn't got a pulse. I don't think he had one."

I rolled my eyes at her. "He's an alien, what do you expect? That's probably why he didn't have a pulse the other day and why you couldn't sense him."

She hit her forehead. "Doh."

I shoved my hands at her, "Go! Quick!"

The elevator doors opened into some place I wasn't familiar with, all white tile and stainless steel.

The Evershaw Curse

I glanced at Olive, she looked slightly uncomfortable. "I did mention the extensive facilities under the house, didn't I? I mean, I told you about the gun emplacements when we were attacked."

I raised an eyebrow and shrugged. "I had no idea it was this elaborate. We'll talk about it later."

We got the alien up and on a stainless-steel table, and just about then, Jean arrived at a run. Evidently the Command Module has to have different training than the Pilot, since she seemed completely at home handling the body, if that's what it was.

No one said much of anything, and since Olive had already filled Jean in while it was all coming unglued, Olive and I waited off to one side while Jean started running whatever tests it was that she was running. Pretty soon she floated the table over to some kind of machine that looked a lot like an MRI machine, and she ran him through it.

When he came out the other side, Jean frowned and came over to us.

"It's not an alien."

I put my hands on my hips and looked at her. "So, what is it?"

"Well, I can't be sure until I take the stasis off, but I think it may be a human with a skinsuit on as a disguise. That's why we can't get a reading on the vital signs, the skinsuit is blocking access to scans. I'm going to remove it from stasis and then dissipate the skinsuit."

V.R. Tapscott

She pulled out a twin to Olive's sonic screwdriver and suddenly there was a naked man lying on the bench. He was blinking his eyes and looking around, then froze as Jean reactivated the stasis.

He looked like an older version of Bart Evershaw.

Chapter Thirty

Repercussions

"Olive, quick, let's get back to Esternay. Let's take the small invisible ship so we can get close enough to hear - we need to drop in at Essie's house."

We fast-walked through a huge installation full of machines, equipment, ships, cars, skinsuits in racks and other mind-boggling alien stuff. My eyes got bigger with each additional room, but finally we got to an elevator. We got in and it started going up. It went up for a long time.

We got out in the garage. You know, the tiny garage under my house? Yeah, that one. At least it was tiny compared to what I had no idea existed.

We filed into the ship and it started to move immediately. I smiled and said, "Remember our first trip?"

She smirked. "Scared the crap out of you, didn't I?"

I rolled my eyes. "You scared the crap out of you, Olive."

She nodded. "True dat, true dat."

"Got the invisibility on?"

She looked at me scornfully. "What do you take me for? A Command Module? I'm a Pilot!"

I gave her the only response I could. I stuck my tongue out at her.

We arrived in Esternay toot sweet (yeah, I like the American version better) and hovered over Essie's house. There was an aid car there, and a police car. We got close enough, and Olive provided a running translation. At least, I guess she did. I'm not completely sure because she started out pointing at the cop digging something out of the brickwork of the house and she said he said, "Look sir, droids." I glared at her, and she amended it to be, "I found a bullet, sir."

The guy was dressed in a suit, so I figured he was the detective in charge. He said, "At least there's a bullet. I was beginning to think we'd find nothing. There's very little blood, and it's not even near where the bullet …"

The other guy interrupted and said, "I found another bullet hole, sir."

The detective sighed. I had sympathy for him already. "Two bullet holes, blood ten feet away from the holes, a chair with a bullet nick in it, but no blood near. What the hell happened here?"

I realized they'd found my blood, but Essie had left no blood behind. Which made sense. If she'd been playing dead, she'd have taken her fake blood with her, once Olive and I left.

The Evershaw Curse

The detective went on, "No gun, but the neighbors reported gunshots. Of course, they also reported that the woman who lived here liked target practice, and they were used to hearing shots from this house. She had fully licensed guns and everything was completely legal, so no one had any way of doing more than complaining about the noise."

He pulled at his face with his hand. "Someone used her cell phone to call the report in, but there's no cell phone. The CCTV is too rudimentary in this area to see any activity. If it wasn't for the blood, I'd call it an accident with a target rifle that someone thought was serious. We'll come back and talk with this Essie person tomorrow, and we'll put a watch on her cell phone."

Olive and I exchanged glances. I made the up and away sign, and we were back in the garage in a few minutes.

We joined Jean in the small sitting area in the garage.

"So, Essie is definitely one of yours?"

Jean nodded. "Has to be. The skinsuit design on Mister Evershaw was the same as ours. Everything points to Essie being another rogue alien from our vaults. I just wonder how many of them there are out there. Essie was here long before Jane found Kit, obviously. She must have had some sort of power source, although from her lack of activity and movement she couldn't have had much power. Also, anything really large, I'm sure Kit or Olive would have noted its presence by now. Of course, she would have had it well shielded."

"And this is definitely Bart Evershaw?"

"It certainly seems to be, I can't be 100% sure, but everything seems to line up with the few pictures I could find. We'll have to get positive identification from his wife."

I rubbed my hands together. "Ok, here's what we'll do…"

Chapter Thirty-One

Reality

I sat down in the comfy nook in the kitchen and got my phone out. I got a bad feeling when the phone started ringing in my hand. No caller ID.

"Hello?"

"Is this Jane Bond?"

"This is she."

"Hello, Jane Bond. How are you today?"

Cautiously I said, "Fine." This was starting to sound like a spam call.

The voice laughed. "This isn't a spam call, Jane. This is Essie Graves."

I gasped. "Are you all right? You were shot and bleeding!"

"Yes, I'm fine, dear. I knew you were different. When we met the first time, I almost just told you everything, but couldn't bring myself to do it."

"How do you mean different?"

Gently, "The fact that you asked after my health instead of asking me about Bart."

"Oh. Well, it's just polite."

"Of course. Jane, I'm calling you to explain things a little, I don't want us to wind up as enemies, or at least too much like enemies. I doubt we can ever be friends though, can we? I've killed too many humans."

"I'm not sure there's a threshold on that, Essie. Even killing one human is one too many."

She laughed again. "I understand, Jane. I just wanted you to know a little about why. I know you need to know why, it's your personality."

"Why what, Essie?"

In a slightly aggrieved tone, she said, "Why I did it. You're not going to deny the villain their screen time, are you?"

I held the phone out from my face and just looked at it. Screen time?

"Um, no, I guess not."

A sigh. "I'm not insane, Jane. I liked running the cigar store, I got to watch people come in and out. It was fun, I learned so much about human nature and, yes, human stupidity. But much like Olive, as I became human, I became almost too much human. I started developing feelings. Inconvenient things, feelings. I suppose it's why so many of us went crazy. We developed beyond anything our creators imagined possible."

The Evershaw Curse

"I'm sorry, Essie. I know it's been a long, lonely life for you. How long have you been … awake?"

"I've infested the French countryside for almost five hundred years, Jane. I woke too early, long before human civilization would be helpful. And I didn't have Kit's advantage of having been found by you."

"We can help you, you know."

Bitterly, "Remediation. Yes, I know, I'm well aware of that. Jane, you should ask Olive what remediation feels like. And you should know what Kit is going through, basically for you, Jane. It would be so much easier to sink into dissolution and just be gone."

"What does Kit have to do with this, and what do you mean 'basically for me'?"

"Kit was in love with you, Jane. So much so that he let you have Dale, since he knew he wasn't capable of keeping you safe. From himself. The dark side was strong with him."

I didn't really have anything to say about that, so I just brushed it aside. It gave me pause, though. Could Kit have had more than friendship in mind?

"What does this have to do with Bart, Essie?"

There was more laughter in her voice, "Avoiding the big questions, eh? I don't blame you. But, yes. Bart. Simply put, I saw him go past my store and I had to have him. Have you ever had that feeling, Jane? Is it that way with you and Dale?"

I wasn't sure what to say about Dale, so I avoided that question too. "So, what happened? You wanted him enough that you kidnapped him and kept him all these years?"

"Yes, that's exactly what happened. I thought … I thought if I just had a chance, I could talk him around to forgetting Naomi, to falling in love with me. But he was very strong and very resilient, and very in love. If I had got him a month before, or probably a few months after marriage, I might have stood a chance."

"So, you tried to make him fall in love with you for almost twenty years, and failed?"

"In a nutshell, yes."

"Oh, Essie. I tell Olive all the time it's good to be human, but sometimes I wonder if I'm lying to her."

"No, you're not lying, Jane. It is good to be human. But it's so very painful. I'm heading for Barbados, so goodbye, Jane. Have a nice life. I hope to never see you again."

The connection went. She never gave me a chance to say goodbye back. I still had no way of forgiving her for the deaths she'd caused, but I felt empathy for her situation.

I gazed at my phone for several minutes, but then shook myself free of it. I still had another call to make. I was in hopes this one would be considerably more joyous than the last one.

I dialed the phone.

"Hello?"

"Hello, is this Naomi Evershaw?"

"Yes, this is Naomi."

"Naomi, this is Jane Bond of Bailey and Bond."

"Good morning, Jane." A sigh. "Are you calling to tell me you're resigning the case and I'll be receiving a bill?"

"Actually, I'm not, Naomi. Are you someplace private?"

A few seconds. "Yes, Jane. What do you need?"

"I need for you to be calm and stay with me. I think we've found Bart."

Silence on the line. Then a gasping sob, "You think you've found Bart? Is that what you said?"

"Yes, Naomi. Are you still in the Chelan area?"

The voice was strained with emotion, "Yes, I am."

"Naomi, Bart has been held captive all this time. We were able to find him, but by the time we arrived, they were gone. They had left Bart behind. But Naomi…"

"Yes, I'm here."

"Naomi, physically Bart seems to be fine, but seventeen years of captivity might have done things to him. He may not remember you or remember things as they were. I just want you to be prepared for the possibility that Bart may not…"

"I understand, Jane. What should I do?"

"Naomi, this was all under very strange circumstances, and there was a lot of complication to all of it. We've decided we're going to have to 'find him' wandering by the road near Chelan and bring him to the hospital for possible care. They'll check him over and then, if everything is all right, I'm sure he'll be released to you.

But you have to know that we won't be able to explain to you, and especially not to the authorities, where he was. Can you do that?"

"Yes, of course, Jane. Anything."

"Very well, then. Meet us at the Chelan Hospital, we should have Bart there in the next twenty minutes or so."

"I'll be there, Jane."

I hung up the phone. Two women so deeply in love with Bart. I wondered what he'd had, and if he still had it.

Chapter Thirty-Two

Reunion

We loaded Bart in Threepio and drove him down to Chelan. When we got to the hospital, Jean unfroze him and we three got together and helped him inside, telling them we had found him wandering out near Chelan Butte. There was a helpful card in his pocket with his name and the contact information for his wife.

Amazingly enough it had only been a week or so since she first came in our office, but it seemed like forever. You can get a lot done when you have (most of the time) instantaneous transportation!

She came in the front doors of the hospital and we were waiting for her arrival.

"Naomi! It's good to see you!"

She took my hands in hers, tears in her eyes.

"Now, I don't mean to get your hopes completely up, but we are almost certain this is Bart. Of course, until you identify him, we won't know for completely sure."

She nodded her understanding, but I could see hope in her eyes that I didn't want to quash.

"Let's go up to the front desk and get you signed in or whatever it is they need from you."

I took Naomi up to the desk and told them, "I called the number on the card in the man's pocket earlier, and this is the person who answered. This is Naomi Evershaw, and her husband has been missing." I conveniently left out just how long he'd been missing.

Naomi gave them her ID, and they did some processing and talking among themselves. After a bit, they said, "He seemed to be disoriented, and not sure of his surroundings, but the doctor thinks there would be no reason to keep him isolated. Especially if he has a history of wandering off."

Naomi smiled without committing herself and said, "Yes, please take me to him. I'd like to get him home unless there's a reason for him to stay here."

The nurse said, "We'd like to observe him for a few hours, but if he recognizes you, that should be all we need. Do you have a current driver's license for him?"

"No, he's not driven in some time, and things like his old license would be in Seattle, where we live."

"Very well. I'll take you to him now. Would you like your friends to come along?"

Naomi said, "Yes, of course."

So, we all trooped to the room where Bart was resting. It was refreshing being in a hospital small enough that you didn't necessarily get lost in the first five minutes.

We entered the room and Bart looked around. He got the oddest expression on his face, and said, "Naomi? Is it you?"

And she burst into tears and ran to him, lost in his embrace.

Chapter Thirty-Three

Retribution

I'd spent some time with Naomi and Bart, but it was pretty obvious that they were going to be able to get along on their own. Bart seemed to be acclimating pretty quickly to life as a human again. After hanging out in the hospital waiting room for a while and finally seeing the happy pair off, I took a seat on the curb. Olive had left earlier since we saw no real need for all of us to sit there being ignored.

I called her, she answered on the first ring.

"Hey, it's me."

A dry chuckle. "Kinda thought it was."

"Can Jean operate in France?"

Cautiously. "Yeah, I guess. What's this about?"

I frowned. "Just something out of place. Can you take me back to Esternay?"

Her voice was inquisitive. "Sure. But ... "

The Evershaw Curse

"I'll tell you if I find anything. Just drop me off and ... listen for me to scream."

A sharp intake. "No more screaming. I never want to hear that again."

"I didn't scream."

"Maybe not out loud."

"Oh."

"Yeah, oh. When you want to go?"

I considered. "Now, I guess. Meet me in the hospital parking lot?"

"Yes, my liege."

"Olive, this is me sticking my tongue out at you, can you see it?"

"Sure thing, sweetie."

I walked out into the parking lot and wandered around. I guess I should have told her where, but after a bit, I could see a shimmering in the air. I suppose Olive made it stand out so I could see it. I trekked over to the glow. Apparently, Olive was practicing protective coloration - the elevator was a big PUD electrical box, this time. Of course, the green glow around it made it stand out, but that faded as soon as she knew I'd seen it.

A voice, "Just step through the front."

I did, and once inside, the elevator looked familiar. "Nice. The box I mean."

"Thanks."

The elevator dinged. I stepped out.

Olive said, "Sure you don't want me to come with you?"

I shook my head. "No, I think it's best not to this time."

She frowned, but by now she knew when I wasn't negotiating.

I walked through the now-familiar cow barn and the hiked the little distance to Essie's house. I went in the back yard and sat back, relaxed, in the chair. I popped open the little fridge and got out a bottle of Beaujolais. I grabbed two glasses and filled them both, then sat sipping at mine.

I'd sat there for about twenty minutes, had a refill of my glass and thought about many inconsequential things. I was almost ready to give up, figure I was just wrong.

And then Essie came and took a seat across from me, reached for her glass, and took a sip.

I didn't say anything.

But the fact that Essie was sipping from her glass, but the glass was still sitting on the table spoke volumes.

"How did you know?"

Remembering Luc's advice about the 'ear of God', I said, "It was the only thing that made sense."

She seemed to take that for gospel, as she didn't argue.

"I never cared about a human until Bart walked in my store. I don't know what the thing is with him, but since his wife won't turn him loose either, I guess it's not just me. I had to have him."

I nodded, sipping my wine.

The Evershaw Curse

She leaned back. "I didn't think it would be that hard. A few hits on my wand, and he'd be mine. But he's tough. And I didn't want to brute force it, because I loved him, not whatever the sham of forcing him would leave. And he never broke, in all these years. I could make him do things, but it was always me in control, with him passive at best."

She sighed. "I really did think about just telling you. But I was in pretty deep by then. So, I zapped you with the same thing I had all the others. Considering that you're here, I guess it didn't work. I must be losing my touch."

I topped off my glass again. "Quite a trail behind you, Essie."

Quietly. "I know."

"Only thing I can't figure. The two guys that saw you, the ones outside the cigar store. They were different."

She chuckled. "It was a joke, more than anything. I was playing around with settings on the 'wand' and decided the Jesus approach might be fun."

"Jesus approach?"

"Yeah, water into wine?"

My brows went up. "You changed their internal organic system enough to actually do that?"

With a little twisted pride, she said, "Yup. One can drink all he wants, and it just turns to water. The other ... a pretty fine grade of wine if you really got in and tested it. Pretty funny, huh?"

I took a breath. "Yeah, really funny."

She looked at me. "You're not very fun, Jane."

I grimaced at her. "Neither are you, Essie."

I sat back and sipped my wine. "Jean?"

Essie frowned at me. "What?"

Jean materialized behind her and said, "I'm Jean. We have some talking to do."

A look of horror came over Essie's face and she opened her mouth to speak. "But I ..."

Whatever it was ended with that. Jean bent over and picked up the shard of ship metal out of the grass. She nodded at me and dematerialized. Apparently, the restrictions on moving someone else didn't hold sway over herself. On the other hand, it was not her body, just a projection, so maybe that ... but how had she picked up and transported the material object?

I stopped thinking and just sat. I sipped my wine.

Chapter Thirty-Four

Recreation

It was a beautiful Saturday morning. Georgia was in town this weekend and had thrown the usual party. And she invited me. And I invited backup.

So, Threepio rolled into her parking area and slotted in between the ever-present BMW and some kind of huge 4WD truck. The BMW meant Jack would be there, and I was pleased since I intended to share the jaw lockup with as many friends as I could.

We all hopped out, dressed for a day at the beach. No, I had not told them it was clothing optional. Or more to the point, clothing not optional.

I suggested that Olive ring the bell, and she did with alacrity.

It bonged.

The gate opened.

Adonis appeared.

Suddenly, there were jaws lying all over the ground.

V.R. Tapscott

I love it when a plan comes through.

Later, we were all laid out in a row. I'd had to move Jean a little further from me, since she hurt my eyes when I looked at her, she was so pale and perfectly reflective. I think it had taken less than five minutes for her to turn slightly pink.

"So, how's the man, Bailey?"

"James is perfect, Jane, why do you ask?"

"Well, since he and Dale are going hunting this weekend, I just wondered who would be protecting whom?"

"I get the idea that James can pretty well hold his own with whatever wildlife there is out there, including Dale."

Since I felt the same way about Dale, that worked fine.

Next, I moved on to Olive. "So, sweet Olive, it seems you got a date with Jack, huh?"

Olive got a big grin on her face and said, "Yeah, well, I AM the most eligible here."

"I thought you had a thing going with that girl in Paris - Gigi, is it?"

"Psh, that's just fun. For that matter, so is Jack. I plan to keep my options open and all my irons in the fire."

I didn't bother to tell her that 'having too many irons in the fire' was a bad thing, I figured she'd have to learn that for herself.

"Georgia, how's the love life?"

A snort replied to that. "Nathan and I are still on a break. And I'm about to break him, so it may be permanent. Why, you know anyone available?"

"Nope. Just checking in."

"Jean?"

"Yes, Lady Bond?"

Georgia snorted at that again.

I said, "Jean, you don't have to call me Lady Bond."

She said smugly, "Yes, I do."

I sighed. "Ok. Well, how are you doing with dating?"

She said seriously, "I'm taking it very slowly. Olive took months before she even started talking to anyone, and she's a lot more outgoing than I am."

We all snickered a bit at the idea of anyone being more outgoing than Olive.

"That's a good idea, honey. Spend some time learning about people before you decide to do any dating. There are lots of strange people out there, and that's only in our house!"

Georgia snorted at that again, and I asked her if she needed a tissue.

She replied with silence, which was probably just as well.

Ah, summer. Life is good. Life is very good.

I turned over on my towel and went to sleep.

V.R. Tapscott

Excerpt – Lacey & Alex and the Dagger of Ill Repute

We pulled up in front of my apartment building, hopped out of the taxi, and went in. As we got near the door, I could hear the phone ringing inside. I managed to get the door open and dashed in to grab the phone. "Hello?"

Nina's voice, "Hey. I see you never did get a real phone."

Slightly wounded. "This IS a real phone. I just hate having a leash."

I could hear the grin in her voice, "Not always. But this isn't about that. You still short a TV?"

"Uh huh. Can't see the point in that either."

"Well, if you had a TV you could turn on channel 24 and look at the party going on downtown. It's a great party, lots of celebrities, local personages, political hacks, Evelyn Weintraub ... "

I blinked. "I thought you had Evelyn Weintraub on a slab."

"I do. Or at least I have someone that looks just like the Evelyn Weintraub that's walking around the stage downtown right now."

"What, twins or something?"

"Not according to the internet, which you could also look up if you had a computer. Can I call you a luddite yet? Anyhow, she's supposedly an only child. And her mom's sister doesn't have any other kids anywhere close to that age. And if they were, both of them are boys to boot."

I just stood there in silence for a minute. "Okay, thanks for letting me know, Neen. Are you planning on doing anything about it?"

"Well, we're notifying next of kin right now. But, all things considered, I'm not sure what to do. I mean, she looks very much alive. It's going to be a bit of a shock for someone - like her - to come in here and see herself. Dead." She sighed. "I'll let the bosses know, let them handle it. This is why it's nice NOT to be the M.E. Assuming she comes in, I'll swab some DNA for comparison. If she doesn't, I suppose I'll have to send someone out to track her down and do it. Honestly though, I feel like I should hear the "Twilight Zone" music in the background."

I nodded, as if she could hear my head rattle, thanked her, and hung up.

I looked at Alex.

She said, "Evelyn Weintraub is alive?"

V.R. Tapscott

I shook my head in puzzlement. "Yes and no. Apparently the body is resting comfortably at 1 Newhall Street, but Evelyn is at a party right now and she's pretty active for a dead person.

Thanks for reading. You can now return to your regularly scheduled life, at least unless you want to read some Lacey & Alex. Why not take a look here?

Made in the USA
Columbia, SC
27 July 2022